PARABLES
OF THE SEA

A VOYAGE OF GRACE, CALLING, AND REDEMPTION

JUSTIN J MAJOR

SEA & SOUL PRESS

Published in the United States by Sea & Soul Press, LLC – Lindale, Texas

seaandsoulpress.com

Printed in the United States of America

ISBN: 979-8-9996068-0-8

First edition

Unless otherwise indicated, Scripture quotations are taken from the Holy Bible, New International Version®, NIV®.

This is a work of fiction. Names, characters, places, and incidents are either the product of the author's imagination or are used fictitiously. Any resemblance to actual events, locales, or persons, living or dead, is purely coincidental.

ACKNOWLEDGEMENTS

This book was not written alone. Every chapter bears the fingerprints of those who prayed, encouraged, challenged, and believed when the waters grew rough.

To my wife and children—thank you for your patience, your love, and the countless evenings you gave so I could pursue the calling God placed on my heart.

To my family, friends, and editor who read the earliest rough drafts—thank you for not running away but leaning in with wisdom and generous feedback.

To my church family and mentors spread across the world—your daily lives have shown me what it means to serve with grace and lead with humility. Your voices echo through these pages.

To the readers, early supporters, and ARC crew who climbed aboard long before the sails were raised—your faith and feedback helped steer this ship.

And above all, to the Captain of my soul—may You find every word in these pages point back to You, the one true Harbormaster.

Thank you for being part of this voyage.

CONTENTS

Before We Set Sail

In the pages ahead, you're invited to enter a world both strange and familiar—a world where life begins underwater, where people move about unaware there's anything more. Everything feels normal. Predictable. Until one day, a glimmer of light pierces the deep drawing you upward. Breaking the surface, you discover another place in this world—brighter, fuller. The same, yet utterly transforming.

I created this world as a way to wrestle with my own questions—about faith, purpose, grace, and the often-challenging path of living as a follower of Christ. In imagining these stories, I found space to explore biblical truths through parable and metaphor, where characters and their journeys mirror the battles we often face, but can't always describe.

As you journey through this world, you may find reflections of your own story. Though these parables were shaped with church leaders, ministry teams, and outreach in mind, the truths they carry reach far beyond titles or roles.

And if you feel like you're still beneath the surface—unsure, unseen, or even stuck—these stories are for you too. There is hope above. A light breaking through. My prayer is that as you read, you will catch a glimpse of that light—and feel its warmth pulling you upward.

PULLED FROM THE WATER

This life underwater is all you've ever known. You didn't choose it, but here you are. Born like everyone else, you come out crying, screaming into this great big world already in motion. You wonder who these people are looking at you and why they are happy to see you. Though for some, happiness isn't the emotion felt. From your earliest moments, you begin absorbing everything—how to move, how to speak, how to survive—without realizing the deep waters you're in. The currents of family, culture, and expectation sweep you along as you begin to grow up.

At first you learn by imitation: how to walk, how to smile, how to hide emotions or mimic false ones. Eventually you're placed into schools where the classes include others like you and the lessons are much more structured. You're taught facts and figures, arithmetic and science, history and various truths shaped by your surroundings. You learn the things placed before you, follow the rules placed upon you and slowly make the long swim toward adulthood. Questions about meaning and purpose bubble up from time to time, but they're soon drowned out by the busyness of life and the need to fit in.

Somewhere along the way, someone mentions another world, an "other place." Maybe it was teacher, a stranger, or simply a story you overhear. The idea of this other place drifts through your mind, but your family doesn't speak about such things. When you bring it up before them, you are given a polite answer, or a dismissive one. You forget about this other place, letting it fade into the background behind more pressing things, like friends, love, ambition, and purpose.

Eventually, you move away from your family and begin choosing your people, your tribe. Together you chase after happiness and success and belonging.

Your tribe says they have found fulfillment, but the more you chase after those things, the more you question why it never feels like enough. Why do you still feel empty after all this time? By all measures of the world you've created, you should be happy and content, but you aren't. You know something is missing.

Then one day something changes. You're walking into work or class or your usual routine when something catches your eye. It isn't a thing exactly, but a light. It shines in a way nothing underwater ever has. It isn't oppressive or demanding, but inviting. Somehow, even though you have no idea what it is exactly, you know what you are feeling from the light is real. You sit in the light, feeling it against your skin. It doesn't burn but warms you deeply. You want to sit in the light, but responsibility pulls you away. Still, the thought of the light and the memory of its warmth lingers in your mind as you lay down to sleep at night.

You tell your friends about the light. Some laugh, while others warn you. They've heard stories about the light and how those who chased after it changed, leaving for another place and never coming back. You nod and listen as each friend shares a differing tale, but your curiosity grows. You need to know what this light is; you need to know about this other place.

The following days and weeks you return again and again to the light. The light doesn't move, but the closer you get, the warmer and more alive you feel. Each time you leave the light the world seems colder and dimmer. You begin to notice just how dark the world really is, not because it changed, but because you did.

One day you decide to touch the light. Just a single fingertip at first, testing the waters. As you brush up against the light, the warmth pushes through your body like every cell in you has come alive. Without hesitation you step fully into the light, and in that moment everything changes.

Suddenly, you are no longer under the surface—you're above it. You're gasping, flailing, tasting real air for the first time. It's both beautiful and terrifying. The water around you is no longer invisible—it's heavy, salty, and foreign. You struggle to breath this new air like a newborn, coughing up years of what you thought was normal. You now know you were drowning all along.

You flail about on the surface trying to stay above the waves, but just as you think you are safe, another wall of water crashes, submerging you again. Salt water floods your lungs, stinging now, where before it was just life. You surface, sputtering and hacking up the water you took in.

Your friends, seeing you struggle, come to help you return to the world you know. They reach for you, not to lift you up, but to drag you back down. They miss their friend and who you were. They think they are saving you, but they don't understand what is happening to you. They hold tight, not wanting to let you go. You try to explain what you saw and experienced on the surface, but they don't want to hear it. You change your plan and instead try to pull them up with you. If they knew the warmth of the sun and the taste of the air, they wouldn't be fighting so hard to pull you down, but they want nothing of it. Finally, realizing your life is at stake, you have to choose. You kick at them as hard as you can, not out of anger, but out of survival. You land solid blows to their faces and arms; they sink back down to the depths, turning away from you, not looking back.

You surface again, hacking and coughing the water back out of your lungs. But there is something new on the surface: a ship is moving across the horizon circling you, large white sails billowing in the wind. A smaller boat with oars approaches. Hanging down, over the side is a man. His hand extends to you. No words. Just an invitation.

You hesitate.

The boat circles back around, the same hand outstretched, patient. You see the face of the man reaching for you, a smile. You reach out, trying to grab the hand, but can't.

"Help me! Grab my hand!" you manage to choke out.

He grabs your hand with a strength beyond anything you've ever known, lifting you up out of the water. The sun hits your skin warming you quickly. You are set down gently onto the deck of the small boat.

The large ship with billowing sails turns to meet the smaller vessel.

You collapse out of exhaustion. You are out of the water, but the journey is just beginning.

When something is all you've ever known—even if it is killing you—it can be almost impossible to imagine anything different. We live in this place, sometimes for our entire lives, unaware we are breathing in a dead world. That is, until we catch a glimpse of something else: a light.

It isn't just any light. This light leads us toward another way—of living, of seeing, of being. While the light feels foreign and new at first, we sense something real in it, something true. Even if we don't fully understand the light, we're drawn to it, we can feel there is substance to the light, there is hope in it.

Jesus spoke of light in Matthew 5:14-16, telling His followers: "You are the light of the world. A town built on a hill cannot be hidden. Neither do people light a lamp and put it under a bowl. Instead they put it on its stand, and it gives light to everyone in the house. In the same way, let your light shine before others, that they may see your good deeds and glorify your Father in heaven."

Simply by living in this world we affect everyone we encounter. Our friends, coworkers, spouses, children, siblings, parents, and even strangers experience something when they interact with us. The light I shine into the world isn't my own, but one I've been given. My role is to reflect it into the world, into the dark depths, hoping that others see it and are guided upward toward the source, toward the surface.

Once at the surface, we all have to make a choice. We decide to call out and reach for that outstretched hand; it doesn't force us. There is nothing any of us can do to make someone take that hand; it is in their control. What we can do is keep shining that light, shining faithfully and intentionally into the depths.

In a dark and disorienting world, the light becomes true north on a compass. A fixed point of reference for those to get back to the surface. The deeper you go, the colder and darker it becomes, and the easier it is to forget which way is up, back to the surface. But the light has the ability to break through, piercing the depths, and illuminating a path back to life. That's why this calling to shine the light is so important. We shine the light not for others to see how bright we can be, but to point others to the surface, to a new world.

A New World

You wake in a small hammock, swaying to the gentle rocking of the ship on the water. The motion is soothing, oddly comforting in contrast to the confusion you begin to feel. Unsure of the last few hours, you lift your head, looking around. A man sits nearby reading a book. You shift and he looks over at you.

"Awake?" he asks, glancing up.

You nod.

"Nothing to worry about. Let's have a look. I'm the ship's doctor." He saves the place in his book and walks over to you.

"Where am I?" you ask.

"On the ship. Do you remember being pulled aboard?"

You nod again.

"Well, it is a ship like many others, out here in your former waters."

"The man who pulled me out?"

"Yes?" The doctor reaches for some water, handing it to you.

"Who is he?" you ask.

The doctor chuckles. "I know that seems like a simple question, but there is so much to Him that it's hard to distill down to a few words. He, at one time or another, pulled each of us from the water."

"You?" you ask.

"Myself included." The doctor reaches over and grabs a small booklet off the shelf. "This should help. Read it when you get a chance."

You thumb through the booklet, glancing at some pictures and reading a few of the words. The doctor waits a moment for you to finish.

"The captain would like to see you if you are feeling up to it."

"I guess." You swing your legs out of the hammock and find your footing.

"Great, follow me. Make sure to use the rails as we go. It is hard early on without them." The doctor leads you down a narrow corridor and up a small staircase. You grip the rails, just as instructed. At the top, a hatch opens onto the deck. The cool air hits your face, and you take a deep breath. The doctor points toward an upper deck where a man stands at a large captain's wheel.

You climb the remaining steps. A broad-shouldered man with a reddish-brown beard stands behind the wheel, holding it on course against the wind and the waves. He smiles as you approach, taking his eyes off the horizon to look you over.

"How are you feeling?" he asks. "Different?"

"I think so. I mean yes, but..." You hesitate.

"You could jump back into the water in an instant?"

"Yes!" you blurt out and then wonder if that was the wrong answer. The captain smiles as he holds fast to the wheel.

"Don't worry. Everyone feels that, some after they have been out of the water a long time. It was home for the better part of your life."

You nod your head in agreement like you understand. You look around the deck, several people are moving about, performing little jobs, keeping up the ship. You keep looking but don't see who you are looking for.

"The man that pulled me from the water, can I see Him?"

The captain thinks about the request for a moment. "In time... You'll see Him again. Don't worry about that."

From the sails above, a young boy comes swinging down onto the deck, letting go in time before flying over the edge of the ship.

"Heya, Cap! Is this the newbie? Nice to meet you. My name's Carson." The boy, maybe twelve, thrusts his hand out to shake yours. You grab it, still in shock from this ball of energy that flew out of nowhere.

"Carson, I'd like you to give the tour of the ship, but you have to promise to slow down. Nobody can understand you when you get like this."

"I can't help it, Cap. I love this, all of it! It is a-mazing." He spins with joy.

"I know, Carson, but please try. Nobody needs to be overwhelmed on their first day."

"Yes, Cap."

Carson grabs your hand and with more strength than you thought possible pulls you toward the stairs to the lower part of the deck. He releases your hand so he can slide down the railing. At the bottom he looks back up at you.

"They tell you about the rails?" Carson asks.

"Yeah, always have a hand on a rail if there is one there, when moving about the ship." You hold the rail as you move down the stairs. "Why is that?"

"The waves can get pretty big at times; the more contact you have with the ship the less chance you have of falling and getting hurt. At least that was what I was told, but it just slows me down."

Carson runs ahead to where a group is washing the deck. He plants his feet and slides on the wet surface till he comes to a stop.

"Carson, did you mend the sails yet?" A new voice rings out, sweet and refined. The woman it belongs to looks up and your eyes meet.

"I'm giving the tour!" Carson responds.

"I'm sure you let the captain know that you hadn't finished your task yet before you agreed to the new one?" Already knowing the response, she asks the question anyways. "I'll keep an eye on..." She looks to you for your name.

You stumble, thinking about your own name, but come back with it.

"Then you can give the rest of the tour," she tells Carson.

"Fine, I'll be back in a flash," Carson reassures you before flying up the nearest mast toward the sails that need mending.

You both watch as he disappears up above.

"That kid is aaa-mmmazing. You can't help but be excited around him, but man can it be draining. I'm Stella," she says, holding out a hand for you to shake.

"Nice to meet you, Stella," you say. "How long have you been...?"

You pause, worried that may not be a normal question.

"Out of the water? A few years now, with this ship ever since," she responds without missing a beat.

"What is this place?" you ask, unsure if it is the right question.

Stella smiles at the question, one she is familiar with herself. "The ship is the *Koinónia*. It floats on the waters of the world you knew. Think of it as two worlds: one below the water and this one above."

"Does it have a name?" you ask, thinking it would be different than what you knew before.

"If it does, I've never heard anything other than the world. It's the same but different. Obviously you can see the big differences: one is wet, the other is dry. You breath oxygen in both places, but one pulls it out of the water around you, while up here you pull it out of the air around you."

You sit down for a minute on a nearby stool, thinking.

"Then why here? Why did he pull me out? Why this place over where I was? Why now? Why me?" You unload a moment, rapid-firing all the questions as they come to you.

Stella sits down next to you.

"You remember asking Him to pull you out?" she fiddles with a small piece of rope lying nearby.

Thinking on it for a moment, you recall the way it all went down, the fresh air, breathing. The outstretched hand that you asked to grab you.

"Yeah, I do." You sit up.

"He pulled you out because you asked Him to. Why you? Maybe you saw the light, maybe you felt the warmth of the sun above. Why the above versus the below?" She stands up and walks over to the railing. "Come stand with me in the sun."

You get up and walk over to the railing with the sun hitting both of you.

"Now close your eyes, and hold your arms out wide," Stella instructs.

You question her with a look but comply with the instructions. You close your eyes and lift your arms from your side to let the sun hit all of you.

At first you feel silly standing there, but the sun begins to pierce into every cell it hits, the energy from it is intense yet soft. It is different, you are different, everything is different.

You open your eyes back up to see her watching you.

"Sorry. There is something refreshing about watching someone experience this for the first time. Not that it gets old for us, but sometimes we forget the wonder of it all." She looks back to the water and the sun.

"All done!" Carson bounds back, panting.

You put your arms down and turn to see Carson half out of breath from hurrying through his task.

"Enjoy the rest of the tour. You're in good hands with this one," Stella says as she returns to the group washing the deck, now toward the bow of the ship.

"Thank you!" you call out after her.

Carson grabs your hand again ready to show you everything you could ever need to know in this new world.

"Come on!" Carson yells, and off he goes, dragging you with him.

An awakening. I'm describing a spiritual awakening, but we've all experienced some sort of an awakening. The information you gained that changed the way you've viewed something the rest of your life. You were one way, you believed a thing, you always did something a certain way, and then it all changed. The purpose of this chapter is to describe how we cross a threshold into a new understanding, a new place mentally, physically, emotionally.

Children—babies even—are masters of awakening. They meet the world with relentless curiosity and no fear of failure. They see everyone walking on two feet, so they pull themselves up and try to walk. They fall, but do they then never try to walk again? No, they fall over and over until they get it, and, as any parent knows, they never stop. They see another way to move through this world, and they want to experience it.

Jesus's encounters with people throughout the Bible were all about this. The woman at the well (John 4), Mary and Martha after Lazarus's death (John 11), and the many He healed whose faith made them whole, each awakened to God's grace, His presence and His love.

But not all awakenings are joyful. Consider Jesus's encounter with the rich young ruler (Matthew 19:16-22; Mark 10:17-27; Luke 18:18-23). The rich young ruler asked Jesus how to inherit eternal life and claimed to have followed every commandment.

Yet Jesus said: "You still lack one thing. Sell everything you have and give to the poor, and you will have treasure in heaven. Then come, follow me."

The rich young ruler walked away sorrowful, awakened to the truth that eternal life was not about checking boxes, but surrendering his heart.

The career man or woman who sacrificed family for the corporate ladder now questions if that is the life they wanted. The young man who realizes his father is not invincible, but human and fallible. The young woman told her value was defined by her beauty and she placed all her effort into it, only to find her worth existed so much deeper, in something that lasts. Such moments can shake us, or save us.

Choosing to always ask questions and be a lifelong learner will set you up to experience many awakenings, both good and bad. It is what we do with the new information that matters most. Learning about the new world you've discovered and your place in it will come with many amazing experiences, memories, and opportunities, but not all of them will be happy. You'll learn things about yourself and others that you may wish you hadn't. And sometimes, you'll come to a crossroad where understanding alone isn't enough. You'll need something more. I call that something *faith,* faith that there is more above the water than below.

Now faith is confidence in what we hope for and assurance about what we do not see.

Hebrews 11:1

THE LIFE BRINGER

Weeks pass and before you realize it, you've been aboard now for over a month, long enough to lose the title of "newbie." It's nice to no longer be the center of attention. The urge to return to the water remains in the background, but you still have so much to learn that you are distracted most of the time. Everything is so new and exciting; it is hard to contain your enthusiasm about the things you've learned and done in such a short amount of time.

You've been shadowing the riggers on the ship, learning everything about the masts, the pulleys, the ropes, and maintaining all of them. Like any new task, it felt complicated at first— everything had a weird name—but you're picking it up and learning.

With time came your sea legs. Moving about the ship became easier, and flying up the masts was like second nature—still nothing like Carson of course, but you could hold your own.

You have friends now too: Derek and Stella, Carson and Thomas, when he isn't in a mood. The captain has taken more time with you than he has with others in the past. You'd been told that is because you ask good questions, but none of them feel that great. They're just things you want the answer to.

Early this morning as the sun had come up over the horizon, you saw a shape flying through the sky off in the distance.

"Derek! Something is in the air," you yell over at your deck watchmate, while pointing toward the spot in sky.

He traces through the air where you are pointing and squints to see what you are talking about. Once he finds it, he knows what to do and runs over to the deck bell, giving it ten rings.

"All hands on deck!" Derek yells followed by ten more rings of the bell.

"What do I do?" you ask Derek after the bell fades.

"When the bird lands, you're going to remove the message it's carrying on its leg, careful not to injure it, then hold it for the captain till he arrives at the helm."

You look back at the giant avian specimen that continues to grow the closer it gets.

The rest of the crew surfaces from below, each moving to their designated spot for a major course correction.

"That's a bird?" you stare in disbelief.

"An albatross, largest bird out here," Derek says as he clears the back deck so it can land. "Be quick about it when it lands and feed it these."

He hands you a small bucket of fish that doesn't smell quite fresh, but you're sure the visitor will enjoy them.

The bird is close, and the shape is apparent now that it is so near. As it approaches, its huge wings begin to push hard against the air to reduce its windspeed. It makes a pass around the boat as if ensuring this is the vessel it was supposed to find. The second pass around it lands right where Derek said it would, toward the back of the ship by the helm. Despite the weight and size of the great bird, its landing is silent.

You place the bucket down for the bird and grab the message tied to its leg. Nervous, your hands shake and untie it, but you get it loose around the same time the bird has finished its bucket of fish.

It looks at you, then at the message in your hand. Satisfied that its job is done, it takes off again back the direction it came.

You watch it as the ship has come alive all around you. The captain climbs the stairs to the helm and watches the bird from behind you.

"What do we have?" he asks, waiting for the message.

You hand it over. He unrolls the paper, reading every word and soaking it all in. A smile comes across his face about halfway through and doesn't leave even after he finishes reading.

"Set a course north-northeast! Get as much wind in these sails as we can." He takes the paper with him as he departs, nodding to Derek as he goes.

Derek takes the wheel and plots the course as you move down to assist your team with the ropes.

Sometime later, the captain reappears from his cabin. He'd changed into workman's garb much like the rest of the crew wore.

"How are we fairing?" he calls to Derek, still at the wheel.

"We've been making fifteen knots when we catch the wind right, but I'd say averaging thirteen," Derek replies.

"Good, good," the captain responds watching the ocean ahead for signs of something. "Should be able to see her soon."

At that everyone moves toward the front of the ship, watching the horizon.

"What is that?" You gasp as the large shape appears far out.

The captain beams for a moment, "That is the *Life Bringer*."

"*Life Bringer*?" You continue to stare into the distance.

"It's a ship," Stella answers. "One of the biggest around. They need our help."

"Again?" Thomas pipes up from the background.

"Now, Thomas, they have the best kind of problem to have," the captain corrects.

Thomas skulks into the background.

Waiting for an answer, you pipe up. "What kind of problem is that?"

"They have more than they can handle!" Carson swings down from the mast. "It's still far out, but I think there are thousands, Cap!"

"You all know what to do. Man your stations!" The captain moves back toward the helm, relieving Derek, and grabs the wheel with both hands. "Derek, I want you to orchestrate the rescues, keep an eye on him." The captain nods toward a sullen Thomas going about his work. "I don't want him getting in His way."

"Aye, Captain," Derek replies.

Like clockwork, everyone scrambles to their stations. Carson climbs back up the mast like he was born there. Several crew members throw rope netting over the sides, and as soon as it unravels, they climb over with it. Thomas, shuffling about, catches Derek's eye.

"Thomas, can you help Doc below? He's going to need help prepping every cot we have. I would appreciate it," Derek requests.

Thomas pauses, wanting to give some reason why this whole event was stupid but decides against it.

"Will do," Thomas responds. He moves below deck to ready cots and recovery stations with everything needed to assist the transition.

You stand, waiting to assist in some way, but feel out of place in the chaos. The captain, seeing you hesitate, says, "Up here. I need your help."

You double-climb the steps to the helm. The captain hands you the wheel.

"Keep us pointed as best you can to that section off their stern, the rear of the ship. We'll anchor there and assist with the rescue." The captain readies himself, saying a quick prayer and moving to the side of the boat to have a better view. Yelling up at one point, "Carson! Keep an eye out for any life rafts. We don't want to run any down."

"Aye, sir!" Carson replies. "Straight ahead should be perfect."

The boat courses through the water, each turn of the wheel bringing it back into alignment where the captain said he wanted it.

As the ship gets closer, the captain handles all the commands to the rest of the crew to take in the sails and prepare to anchor. The life rafts surrounding the giant ship are moving about picking up more people reaching out of the water.

"There!" the captain yells, pointing toward a life raft without anyone in it yet, manned by a single individual.

The crew lets out the sail to gain a little speed toward the raft before taking the sails back in. The crew on the anchor drops it to lock the ship in place.

You move down, closer to the edge where the nets went over, watching the crew members set up a makeshift dock that floats next to the side of the boat. A ramp leads up into the side of the ship where the recovery cots are.

"Down here!" the captain yells up to you.

You climb over and move down the netting to the platform.

"I need you to climb across this plank to his raft and help hoist the people in that He has grabbed."

They lay a plank across the gap, and you look unassured at the stability of the makeshift bridge.

"You'll be fine. Hurry across now." The captain helps you step.

You place one foot in front of the other, trying not to focus on the ocean below. Before you know it, you are across and in the boat, staring into the face of the only man on the raft.

"How can I help?" you say, not knowing what to do.

"Any minute now, they'll start surfacing. Be ready to assist them into the boat when they do," the young man says.

You watch the water in anticipation, unsure where the first one will be. A bubbling starts near one side of the boat and then another, and before you know it, there are bubbles all around the boat.

Over the edge, you hear the first one. "Please help me," the young woman says.

Without any warning, He is there in the boat with the two of you. The same one Who pulled you from the water. He reaches down and grabs her hand. You help her into the boat from there, grabbing a blanket to wrap around her, trying to help her dry off and get her warm.

Another one calls out from the water, and He again reaches for the hand of the next and pulls a young man into the boat. The young man and woman know each other and hug each other crying together as they share the blanket.

These two lead to several more coming out of the water, old and young alike. He grabs one hand after another pulling them into the boat. You begin readying some of them to cross the same small plank back to the ship, ensuring they can walk fine and someone on the other side can assist them.

You lose count at one point and focus on caring for those in the boat. When it is all said and done, you are exhausted, helping what felt like 150 people transition from the water. You slip down into the boat, collapsing for a moment. The young man in the boat does the same thing.

The One Who pulled them all out stands at the end of the boat smiling back at the two of you nodding His head in thanks.

"I'm Collin, by the way," the young man says, and you both laugh realizing you never exchanged pleasantries. You share your name with him and sit for a bit. Looking back to the end of the boat you see He is gone, the one Who pulled them out.

"Is that all then?" the captain hollers.

"Yes, sir. Collin and I were just taking a moment," you reply.

"Collin! Is that Maureen's boy?" the captain asks.

Collin stands up.

"Aye, Captain. The same." He beams, a knowing nod and silent exchange between them.

"That's good then, Collin. Truly great to see you." The captain nods again and departs back up the side of the ship to the deck.

"We need to get moving, see who else needs help," Derek calls to you.

You look to Collin, who nods for you to go. You move toward the plank to leave.

"If it only saves one," Collin says as he holds out his hand to shake.

You grab it unsure if there is something else you are supposed to do.

"It'll be worth it," Derek says, finishing the ancient reply for you.

"It is worth it," you say and head across the plank back to the ship, waving goodbye to Collin as he rows on to see where else he is needed.

Have you ever had the opportunity to be a part of something bigger than yourself? A moment where people united under a shared mission, setting aside personal goals for something greater? That's what this chapter captures: the beautiful surrender of our individual callings, at least for a time, for the sake of a larger one.

It's a truly selfless decision to put aside your own mission to assist others in theirs. This recognition that another person's purpose aligns with ours, and if their mission's fire is already burning hot and bright why wouldn't we throw our wood on their fire—rather than trying to build our own.

When we lived in Virginia, our church had the means to create several social programs for the community—but chose not to. Why? Because many already existed nearby and were run exceptionally well. So instead, we partnered with them. Partnering with the local food pantry, we dedicated entire services to supporting them. We would meet, be encouraged, and then head out to buy non-perishables, returning with carloads for a semi-truck headed to the pantry. We knew we wanted to help the community, and we found organizations that aligned with us in that mission. We also didn't need our name being on a banner with the organization, because it wasn't about the recognition or our ego. It was about the mission.

The final sentiment of this chapter is that a single life changed makes any amount of effort worth it. That is how I feel about this book. If a single sentence or chapter helps someone navigate a storm in their life, then the writing was worth it. But of course, we hope for more—dozens, hundreds, generations changed.

The mission of the ship was to help transition people to this new life—a mission that the *Life Bringer* shared. When called upon to help, the captain answered without hesitation because he knew it served the mission of not only the *Life Bringer*, but of him and his crew and ultimately the One who sent them, the Harbormaster. Helping a single person in their most vulnerable moment step into something new and better—whatever that may be—is what we all should aspire to.

Do nothing out of selfish ambition or vain conceit. Rather, in humility value others above yourselves, not looking to your own interests but each of you to the interests of others.
Philippians 2:3-4

Man Overboard

The elation and excitement from the previous day's rescue still pulses through the ship. Joy hums in the conversations, in the shared meals, in the way the crew moves. Attention has shifted from you to the newcomers and their stories—each one a miracle in its own right. Some of their lives are much like your own, while others' experiences bring the crew to tears. The fact that some of these people had been through so much and were still standing amazes. One guy described his encounters with the great beasts of the ocean, and he showed the scars to prove it. Deep jagged lines marked his body from head to foot where the creatures had made every attempt to end him, but here he was alive, sharing with the crew.

Toward the edge of a small gathering sits another newcomer, silent, wrapped tightly in a blanket. He was listening, but his attention was held more by the water than the tales everyone shared. You had some idea of the thoughts racing through his mind. Though there's everything new ahead, the pull of everything below—the familiar, the formative—still lingers. You understand and remember that feeling.

Without warning, he stands, dropping the blanket from his shoulders and leaps into the water.

You dive in after him.

"He was so close to the surface," you say, coughing up water as the crew wraps you in towels. "I was only trying to help him get back to the surface."

The crew, still silent, listens while you work through the situation.

"I mean, that is what we are supposed to be doing, right? Getting people to the surface."

One of the older crew members rubs his stubbled chin before piping up. "You went back into the water to do it though. You aren't ready for that."

"Very few ever are." The captain nods to the crew, and they move back to their jobs on the deck. He sits down next to you.

"But we are supposed to be helping. There are thousands—hundreds of thousands down there. If we can't go get them, how will they ever find the surface?"

You bury your face in the towel you were given, wiping the salt water out of your eyes and hair.

"I could drop you back in the ocean today," the captain says. "You could spend your life trying to coax people upward. But that's not how it works. Immersion is a dangerous thing. You'd be living, but it is only a matter of time: not *if* you'll go under, but *when*. When will a great beast come along and devour you whole? When will the water hit your lungs again? And when it does, will you be able to spit it out—or will you sink into what you once escaped?"

"But I'm different now. I could never go back there like none of this has happened."

A sorrowful smile comes across the captain's face. He reaches into his shirt pocket and pulls out a pocket watch. Upon opening it, you can see there is a picture inside of a young boy.

"My son." He shows you the picture. "He joined the crew at seven and grew up right here on this ship, knew it as well as I do. One day while I was looking over some charts..." Tears gather in the captain's eyes. "He jumped right over the side. At first, I thought he may have been doing what you just tried, but when we ran over to see, he was gone."

"Why did he do that?" you ask.

"*Why*," the captain speaks the word, knowing it all too well. "It is the question of all questions, the one that is hardest to answer, and it feels like the most important."

The captain closes the watch and tucks it away.

"I've spent years replaying that moment. I remember his eyes on the water, watching it move, at least I thought."

"It is beautiful," you suggest. "It is creation and chaos, beauty and disaster, all at once."

"It is, but his gaze was..." The captain closes his eyes. "I can see him on the railing staring into the ocean, but he isn't staring. He is looking for something, peering deeper."

The captain's eyes shoot open; the past too painful to dwell in for long. "It seems obvious now, but I missed it when it mattered."

Silence fills the gap before you speak again. "Do you know where he is now?"

"I know exactly where he is."

Surprised, you look up at the captain. "What do you mean. If you know where he is, why aren't you there?"

"I have my orders." The captain sighs, restrained. "And they don't include waiting around for my son."

"But—how can you...?" You're confused.

"Because I trust. It's complicated and doubt plagues me, but at the end of the day, in the dark as I am lying down to sleep, I regain a peace. I *feel* this is where I am supposed to be, and I have faith that everything else will be taken care of in time." The captain stands. "That is enough for now. Finish drying off and see Arthur about a pack. He'll load you up with supplies."

"A pack? Am I going somewhere?"

The captain smiles. "We'll be in port first thing tomorrow morning. The next part of your journey is about to begin."

You can't save them all. Truthfully, you can't save anyone. Take *save* to mean whatever you like: helping someone change, showing them another path, offering a better way to live. You can lecture, listen, teach, coach, help, encourage, plead, pray, drag, or even carry someone. But you can't make them change.

We want to help. We *should* want to help. But if you've spent any time trying to rescue others—truly rescue them—you've already learned this: effort alone isn't enough. Our love isn't enough. Our sacrifice isn't enough. Not when someone isn't ready to change.

And many *want* to change. They want to come out the other side a better person, and they'll pay good money for it. There is a multi-billion-dollar industry thriving on this. But no amount of training, coaching, educating, or even hand-holding can do for them what they need to decide for themselves, that they want to change.

In Matthew 13, Jesus described this reality in the parable of the soils. The same seed is scattered—same sower, same message, same life-giving truth. But the results vary wildly based on the soil (state of the person) they fall on. Seeds scattered across all kinds of soil, but only the good soil bore fruit. Not everyone is good soil—yet. And we can't force them to become good soil.

So how do we know when someone is good soil?

The truth is: you don't always know. Not right away. But there are always signs.

Good soil *receives*. It's soft enough to let the truth in. You'll see it in the tears after a hard conversation, in the questions that come after, in the way they stick around when it would be easier to run.

Good soil *retains*. It doesn't just feel something—it holds onto it. Holding fast to the truth it has been given, maybe even wrestling with it, but not letting it go.

Good soil *responds*. Change begins to happen. It isn't always immediate, and it requires patience, but roots are being formed. There is growth.

So, what do we do with this parable? How then are we supposed to act?

We focus on the mission God has called us to. We pour into the people we've been entrusted with: the parent determined to be the best version of themselves for their kids; the leader who becomes a "Ted Lasso" to their team, always encouraging and helping; the friend who shows up again and again for the one who needs stability and someone they can trust.

But sometimes—like in our parable—we realize no amount of help will reach someone until they are ready. So, we work with those who are ready. Those who have done the heart-work.

We don't forget the others. We watch and wait. And when they rise—we're there. Ready to help them in the boat, ready to help them into this new world.

LIFE ON SHORE

The ship docks early in the morning as the sun peeks over the horizon. You didn't need to be woken—your excitement and anticipation kept you up most of the night. As such, you are already on the deck as the ropes are thrown to moor the ship. You said your goodbyes the night before, but still, several members of the crew are there to see you off, including Carson who, despite his normal energy, struggles to fight against the early morning pulling on his eyelids.

You thank the captain once again before disembarking.

"Any last advice?" you ask.

"The second you were rescued you became a rescuer. Don't forget that. The land has a way of making people forget. We were all rescued and now we're rescuers—first and foremost." The captain leaves you with a strong pat on the back and that wisdom.

"Thank you, Captain," you say as you step off the ship for the first time.

As you walk down the dock, unease begins to rise in your stomach.

Was this a test? you think. *Was I supposed to choose to stay on the ship, and I've already failed? Or was I up before all the others who were supposed to depart the ship today?*

You look back. No one else is disembarking yet.

"New to the port?" a kind voice calls to you.

You turn to look and see an older woman smiling at you.

"Yes," you say, moving toward her. "Just got in, but the captain gave me this."

You hand her the two envelopes the captain had given you for your departure.

She reviews them carefully, handing them back as she describes them.

"This will get you lodging for the first month you're here. And this one"—she pauses, holding up the envelope sealed with gold wax—"this is for the Harbormaster's eyes only."

She looks back toward the town, trying to find something and then waves to a young boy.

"Rickson! Delivery for you," she calls over to him.

He comes jogging over, with almost the same energy as Carson, but much more well-mannered.

She begins to hand him the envelope for the Harbormaster.

"Wait. Should I take it?" you ask.

"You can if you'd like, but this is Rickson's job just the same." She points out a lapel pin you hadn't noticed before bearing the same seal as the envelope.

"I suppose that is fine. Thank you, Rickson," you say.

Rickson takes off running with the delivery into the town.

"And thank you..." you say wondering her name.

"Maggie, or Miss Maggie, is what you'll hear some people call me around town, or if you make your way to my place, The Retreat, for a drink." She sticks out her hand to shake and you oblige.

"Thank you, Maggie. Where is the lodging you mentioned?"

Maggie points as she explains. "Straight down this street till the end. You'll see several shotgun shacks. Mr. Carter is in the blue house and will get you taken care of."

"Thank you," you say as you start walking the way she directed.

The harbor town was waking up, and the smells of fresh baked bread and rashers of bacon fill the streets. A man outside the bakery carrying a tray of biscuits looks you over.

"Just get in?" he asks.

"Yes," you respond.

He tosses you a warm biscuit as he continues down the street.

"Best in town. Come by after you get settled if you need work," he says as he is walking away.

Several others stop you on your way to greet you and offer unsolicited assistance on where to find things and what jobs are available.

You make it to the end of the street and over to the blue house.

Mr. Carter is as kind as Maggie, if not kinder, showing you the small, one-room shack you'd be calling home for the time being. The word *shack* didn't do the house justice. It was clean and well kept, warm and welcoming, just small. Plenty of room for you though.

You sit on the bed, reflecting. You've come so far. You think about the time that has passed since you surfaced. So much to process still, guilt over being here in the light and the friends and loved ones who aren't yet. You remember the captain's story about his son and the captain being where he was supposed to be. You wrestle with the thought, unsure if the captain's words bring any comfort knowing your family is still out there in the deep.

A big blank future sits before you. Excited and scared all at the same time, you remember what the captain told you. You are a rescuer now.

"But who am I supposed to rescue?" you say out loud to yourself.

KNOCK, KNOCK! The door sounds almost in reply to your question.

You get up to answer the door.

Rickson stands at the threshold.

"The Harbormaster would like to speak to you, if you have a moment?" he says.

"Um... sure." You look back at the house that isn't going anywhere wondering if you should bring anything.

"You can leave all that. I'll take you," Rickson reassures.

You follow Rickson back through town, down several streets you hadn't seen before, eventually heading uphill toward what seems to be the town center. A large building sits against a serene backdrop of the harbor.

Rickson opens the door and ushers you in. In the middle of the room sits a large desk with several stacks of papers and barrels full of scrolls piled about. The shelves around the room are stacked deep with even more papers. Charts and charters hang out from every place in the room.

Behind the desk sits a strong, stout older gentleman. Clean-shaven but weathered, He looks up from the desk at you and a large smile crosses His face. Grabbing at the paper and envelope that bore His seal, He gets up to greet you.

"Finally, we meet." He greets you with a huge hug like a friend that hasn't see you in years.

"Finally? Maybe you have the wrong person, I just got here," you say, surprised by Him.

"I think not!" He says, smiling at Rickson, who smiles back with a gleam of understanding in his eyes. "I saw you in the depths and knew you. I've been waiting for you."

You see the sincerity in His eyes and know He is speaking the truth, as strange as it seems.

"Well, here I am," you muster in the odd exchange.

"Here you are indeed. Sit, sit." He ushers you to a chair across the desk from Him, and He sits back down in His.

Still holding the papers in His hand, He smiles as He looks at them again.

"Is that what you wanted to see me about?" you ask.

"Yes, in a way," He says looking back at the shiny pages, glimmering in the sunlight pouring through the glass ceiling.

"May I see it, sir?" You sit up to take the pages.

"I'm afraid not." He puts the pages back into the envelope. "That is what will be, and it makes me happy. But if I showed it all now, I fear you wouldn't understand—or worse, you'd quit before you even began."

"I don't understand. What will be?" you say.

He sits back in His chair looking you over.

"So very good to have you here. But if you aren't too busy already, I have something for you to do. A mission of sorts." He shuffles through the papers on the desk looking for something.

"A rescue mission?" you ask, wondering if this was the answer you were looking for.

"Perhaps," He replies as He finds the papers.

Papers of Commission it reads at the top.

You sit, waiting as He fills them out, double checking all the elements of the commission.

"Very good," He says as He finishes, sealing it with wax and handing them over to you. Getting up from His chair, He ushers you toward the door. "Good luck! And don't hesitate to ask questions if you should have any. The harbor is here to help."

With that, He pats you on the back and sends you on your way, closing the door behind you.

You meander back to your house, retracing the path Rickson led you down.

You close the door behind you when you arrive and sit down at the small table, setting the orders in front of you.

"Well, that was fast," you say as you break the wax seal on the commission.

There are two ways to live: actively or passively. You can choose to let the ocean take you wherever it would like, or you can trim your sails and head into the great unknown with a purpose. The problem people have is that they get into a rhythm of busy where they would say they are very active but aren't actually moving in any direction. They move through their days but don't actually go anywhere.

Becoming a rescuer—that takes action. It is a choice. The act of rescuing is not one of passivity, but of action. Storming the castle takes action, defending the fortress takes action, running into a burning building takes action, forgiving someone takes action and asking for forgiveness takes action.

This life on shore can be one of the most dangerous things for all of us. It is safe and comfortable. That's the danger. We forget our purpose. We forget the rescue.

Many Christians forget the Great Commission. They explain it away and say how that wasn't for them, but rather, for others who are called to be missionaries. They delegate to others, maybe giving a little money to a cause, but never seeking out the lost themselves. Now don't hear me wrong—generosity is good—but if that is all you do, it's like you've taken your orders from the Harbormaster and buried them in the junk drawer in your little shack. You've chosen passivity. You've exchanged calling for comfort.

James 4:17 says, "If anyone, then, knows the good they ought to do and doesn't do it, it is sin for them."

What commission have you set aside? What calling have you postponed? To be the best spouse your partner deserves? The parent your children need? The friend, the leader, the disciple? I don't know what your thing is, but I can tell you it isn't contingent on anyone else's action but your own.

Find that commission that you hid away, dust it off, read it again. Now stand up and take action. Grab those orders and run to the port. You have work to do.

The Empty Berth

You have your orders. With excitement, you set out for your berth in the port only to arrive at an empty space at the dock. You open your orders again, reading them with great care. Nowhere do they mention the vessel you are to use to complete your mission. A wave of worry sweeps over you.

Do I have to build the boat as well?

You sit on the edge of the dock, scanning the pages again, unsure if you missed something. Across the way, you see a young man arrive at another section of dock with his own papers in hand. Waiting for him is a small ship already prepared for the journey. A small crowd from town gathers to send him off. They give him hugs, supplies, and encouragement before he jumps aboard and sets sail for the horizon.

Bitterness sweeps over you as you watch him sail away.

Why was it so easy for him? Does he even deserve that boat? Did I get the wrong orders? Am I at the wrong dock? What if I'm not capable?

Shoulders heavy, you pick yourself up and walk to the Harbormaster's office. Your three gentle knocks on the door are answered by a bellowing, "Come in!"

You take your hat off as you walk inside, papers are scattered about the Harbormaster's desk, each one exactly where it belongs.

Without looking up, He says, "Here so soon?"

"About my orders."

He finishes writing with the quickness He is accustomed to and seals the papers, another set of orders. He hands them to a young boy, half Rickson's age, who is waiting for them. The boy runs out the door prepared to deliver the orders. A young girl takes his place ready to deliver the next set.

He pauses and looks up at you, a smile comes to His face. "You know I tell everyone to ask questions, but most people don't. They either don't carry them out, or they sit there fumbling about thinking they are all alone in this endeavor. What do you need to know?"

"There's no boat."

"I know."

The silence hangs in the room, finally cut by a giggle from the young girl. The Harbormaster smiles at her and sends her out.

"But these orders require a boat."

"I know," He repeats with a smile.

Frustrated, you drop into the chair before His desk.

"I watched another young man get to his spot at the dock and a brand-new ship was waiting for him."

"He built it." The Harbormaster lights a pipe and sits back in His large leather chair.

"But I saw him arrive with his orders. They were new."

"Do you need orders to build a boat?" He asks between puffs.

The weight of His last question sinks in. "No, I suppose not."

He smiles again. "He believed orders would come. So, he started building. Don't feel bad. Whether you already built a boat or not doesn't matter. I've seen men build fantastic ships only to watch someone else captain it out of the harbor. What matters is you're here—and you're willing?"

"Yes, sir." The original excitement of getting your orders is back.

"Good. Your orders are the guide. Go out into the community, seek those who have had similar orders in the past, and consult them on the make and build of their boats—the things they wish they had, the things they didn't need. Lastly, with your plan in hand, share it with the community. You'll be surprised who shows up to help."

The orders are finally here. Your mission—the thing burning inside of you—that you want to share with everyone that'll listen. It is finally here.

But now what? In the story, you head down to the dock and find your slip empty. No boat in sight. No plan. Yet the stirring in your chest is unmistakable. You've been asking for this thing for what feels like ages, and when it shows up, you feel unprepared. You've sat idle, waiting for answers instead of positioning yourself for the opportunity.

Here is a freeing truth: many different paths through life exist simultaneously within God's will for you. We all have a myriad of choices in this life. Going to college or not, working at that Fortune 500 or starting your own business, getting married or being single, kids or no kids... The list goes on with countless paths to take, but where so many people go wrong is they think there is a single perfect path for their life. Christians may talk about "God's Perfect Plan" for their life and wanting to know exactly what that is before moving in any direction. But it isn't a plan, it is plans, plural. Jeremiah 29:11 says, "'For I know the **plans** I have for you,' declares the Lord..." An omniscient God doesn't sit there and see a single perfect path. He sees them all, both the paths we could take that bring Him great joy and paths that lead us away from Him. For all of us, since we don't have this ability, this feeling we get about messing up a plan comes from a place of fear. We don't want to make a mistake and "ruin" the rest of our life because we went down a path that wasn't the "perfect" one. God knows what you will choose to do, but free will—the same free will that allows you and I to decide to believe or not believe—carries over into our life choices.

The following should help sort through those fears of making a wrong decision.

When you were pulled from the water, you were given your first and permanent order: to be a *rescuer*.

With that in mind, every decision and path moving forward should support that calling. Any paths that take you away from that act, counter to your orders, and we know it isn't the right path for us. It may still be the right path for others, based on their calling, so long as they are acting as a rescuer. Too often we think because a path wasn't right for us, that it shouldn't be right for anyone else.

But ultimately what we mean is that this path, this choice, didn't align with the additional orders we have.

Once you embrace your role as a rescuer, you can start moving—even if you don't yet have detailed orders. The young man across the dock started building long before he knew the mission. And when it came. He was ready.

Can a rescuer be married? Single? A parent? A CEO? A teacher? Yes, yes, yes, yes, and yes. If you're making rescuer choices, I will be bold and say God is with you.

Acts 13:22 says, "...God testified concerning him: 'I have found David son of Jesse, a man after my own heart; he will do everything I want him to do.'"

Be that person. Chase the heart of God. Live life as a rescuer first and everything else will take care of itself.

The Tale of the Rudder, the Rope, and the Wheel

The salt water laps against the boat you're building, splashing as you test the buoyancy with the old shipwright. A bit of the salt spray hits his face and lips.

"Salt," he mutters, spitting. "I hate the salt."

"What's that?" you ask.

"My first assignment—there was a storm... Salt spray stung my eyes. I'd close them to escape it. Thinking myself safe, I'd try to open them, only to have another wave cover the deck again. As hard as the storm tried, the boat popped back up on top of the water again and again. The captain was at the wheel, turning the ship with each wave to try and gain relief from the relentless beating the ship was taking."

"Were you scared?"

"How could I not be? I'd seen these storms from the shores and felt what they could do, how they could change entire landscapes," the old shipwright says as he marks spots on the inside of the vessel that appear damp.

"What happened?" you ask, intrigued by the story.

With that the old shipwright's story begins.

The wind blasts the ship while the waves crash over its sides, battering the hull from what seemed like every direction.

The old shipwright, much younger, runs the deck, tying down the ropes and securing what he could before returning to the helm with the captain.

"Boy, help me pull the wheel!" the captain shouts at the young shipwright.

He jumps into action, helping turn the wheel, making ground on it, if only by an inch at a time. He tries to get the ship to turn into the large waves heading right toward them. Without the sails, it felt useless.

The waves roll onto the ship, almost pushing it over into the water before righting itself back up only to be battered again and again.

"More! Pull harder! We got to get her turned!" the captain yells.

A few more crew members come to help pull on the wheel. With all their combined might, it begins to turn where the captain needs it to be.

With a loud snap, the tension releases and everyone on the wheel falls to the deck as the wheel spins without control.

"It broke!" The captain's yell feels like a whisper against the storms raucous howls.

Everyone looks to the captain for guidance in that moment as it appears hope is lost.

"Man the bilge pumps. Keep the water out and be johnny-on-the-spot looking for leaks. We're gonna take a beating while we get this fixed, but we have everything we need. Hop to it!" The captain spouts off a confident list to the crew, who jump right up and move to the areas needed.

The captain grabs the young shipwright and says, "I'll need your help running the rope through for the tiller. We have a replacement in the hold. Go get it."

The young shipwright darts with a flash, running down the deck to get below, but a large wave pummels the deck, engulfing the young shipwright and dragging him to the other side of the deck, almost over the side into the water. As the wave slips off the deck, the young shipwright vomits salt water onto the deck only to watch it slip off the edge back from where it came.

The shipwright gulps a big breath of air and continues moving across the deck down the stairs below. Several men and women are patching holes the storm has already caused, and the pumpers are working as fast as they can clearing water. Everyone is doing their part.

The young shipwright shimmies through the hold looking for the rope to replace the tiller rope, but the hold is filled with all sorts of items. The stacks of ropes of all sizes are tangled together and unkempt. Without a label or sorting system, it is hard to tell where one begins and another ends. The sizes of the ropes are all he has to go by, and he tosses some aside as they are much too small to be the right one. Above, he can hear the captain yelling orders.

"Where is that rope? Tell him to feed it up to me."

The young shipwright plows through the ropes, tossing the smaller ones aside. Buried underneath the stack he sees a newer rope roughly the same size as the rope wrapped around the barrel of the wheel. He grabs it and throws it on his shoulder as he heads to the back of the ship where he can feed it through the floor to the captain.

"Please let this be the right one," the young shipwright whispers as he begins feeding the rope up through the floor to the helm.

"Good work!" the captain yells down. "The new rope needs to run through the pulleys where the old rope is and then fix it to both the starboard and port sides!"

"Aye, aye!" the young shipwright yells back in return.

Another crew member shows up, the one ordered to see what was taking so long. The young shipwright hands the other end to her, and they pull the new rope through where the old rope had been, feeding it through the pulleys as they pull the old rope out. They pull the rope through an additional set of pulleys affixed to the wall of the ship and then back to the tiller pulleys.

They are bashed back and forth as the waves spin the ship, but they finish running it through the pulleys and fix it to eye screws on either side of the ship.

"Captain! We're fixed," the young shipwright shouts up, but no reply comes.

The young shipwright runs through the hold back up the stairs getting to the deck. The captain is up top but lying over the wheel unconscious.

"Captain!" he yells.

The young shipwright fights the waves across the deck and up onto the helm, pulling the captain off the wheel and laying him on the deck, careful not to knock his head.

"I need help up here!" the young shipwright yells down.

He takes the wheel, turning back into the waves as best he can against the storm. The new line feels different than before, strong, resolved. The ship moves much easier with each turn.

The female crew member who helped secure the new tiller rope appears up the stairs.

"Get him below! I don't know what happened," the young shipwright shouts over the storm.

She grabs the captain and drags him down, other members of the crew arriving to help get him to his quarters.

The waves bash the young shipwright as he holds fast to the wheel, spitting out the salt water.

"Come on! Is that all you got?" he yells into the storm.

With that, the old shipwright's story ends.

"Why'd it snap? Too much pressure from the waves?" you ask as you point to other damp spots on the hull of your new boat.

"Or just old and weathered. The rope takes your commands at the wheel and transfers them down to the tiller and ultimately the rudder. Over time the rope can wear thin, become frail and faulty due to any number of things if it isn't maintained and refreshed often." The old shipwright, happy with the markings made, points over to the rope to haul the boat back out of the water. "I've heard stories of ships sailing off the ends of the earth never realizing that their tiller rope is broken, riding on forever into sunset after sunset, oblivious of the fact they have no control until it is too late.

"You made it."

He looks up at you.

"I did, but what I remember the most about that day is how much salt there was. I'm fine never tasting a mouthful of salt water ever again."

Direction. We all want it. We pray for it. We plead for it. Then when we receive the direction we seek, we have to do something about it, we have to act.

A sailing vessel's basic movement system has a captain's wheel wrapped in a rope, the tiller rope, which connects to the tiller, a lever that acts against the rudder, changing the ships direction.

If the wheel is your decision to move or act. The tiller is your beliefs, convictions, and habits. The tiller rope? That is your resolve. It transfers desire into action. But regardless of the desire to move and the strength of your beliefs and convictions, if your resolve is weak, the movement can fail.

Additionally, outside forces can apply pressure to the rudder forcing movement through the system from the opposite direction. How many times have our convictions and beliefs been challenged by outside forces? This pressure ultimately moves further into the system challenging our resolve. As was the case in this story, the turmoil in the sea challenged the force put into the system by all at the wheel and actually destroyed the weakened tiller rope.

To avoid this, the tiller rope, your resolve, should constantly be going through a transformation—or renewal. Romans 12:2 says, "Do not conform to the pattern of this world, but be transformed by the renewing of your mind..."

As Christians we need to ensure we are allowing time for renewal. Whether intentionally or not we develop habits and principles that affect our resolve. If shaped by Scripture, by prayer, being in community with other believers—resolve strengthens. If shaped by the world—resolve weakens. Taking time away to diligently strengthen one's resolve is critical.

Jesus knew when to step away. Most notably in His desire to have quiet time with God, He would go off by Himself while people still wanted to talk to Him. He recognized how critical that time was for Him, just as it is for all of us.

We also strengthen our resolve by finishing what we start. Completing goals, sticking to decisions, doing the hard thing—all of these establish benchmarks for what we know is possible. Then when faced with new challenges we have a library of experiences to pull from and relate to. We can see, because I was able to accomplish this goal, I should be more than able to do the next. Your resolve strengthens.

I wish it was as easy as deciding to move, turning the wheel, and the ship turns exactly where you want it to go. Unfortunately, there are infinite factors at play. Not always our own issues, but figurative storms, headwinds, currents, a myriad of other things affect our trajectory too. With all of these outside forces at play we have to pay special attention to the only thing we can control—our steering system.

Examine your system:

- Wheel: Are you taking the right action?

- Tiller Rope: Is your resolve strong?

- Tiller: Do your beliefs, habits, convictions align?

- Rudder: Are outside forces shifting your direction?

Move through the system checking every piece to identify any outstanding issues. Fix what is necessary. A quick note: fixing issues is much easier when the inside of your ship is clean and decluttered. The story spoke of piles of ropes lying mixed together in the ship. There is a whole other chapter to be written on that element, but just know it will serve you well to keep your ship sorted.

The fastest way to test this is to take the wheel and start making moves. Hopefully you'll find a steering system in perfect working order—a ship moving exactly where you are called to be. But as is often the case you will likely find problem areas in your system and can address those accordingly.

Either way you have to start making moves. Grab the wheel, and let's get moving!

THE MISSION TO THE SHALLOWS

The seas are calm this morning and the air fresh. Several gulls sleep along the docks as the morning sun peeks over the horizon. Your maiden voyage would be without fanfare or trumpet; the kindly old shipwright who helped you construct the boat stands along the dock waiting for you. As you reach him, he puts a steady hand on your shoulder and squeezes.

"Remember the teachings, and you'll do fine. Don't try so hard to reason through it; leave room for the Harbormaster's words," he reminds you.

You nod in understanding and settle into your small boat.

"One last thing," he says, as he hangs a lit lantern on the hook at the front of the boat. "Keep it lit, and let it shine."

You smile at the small lantern casting a bright light in the morning haze. Sitting there in your boat you pause.

"Is the boat too small?" you ask, too late to make a difference.

"We'll see," he says with a shove.

You set the oars to pull yourself out of the harbor. The old man waves you off and returns to his chair at the dock. Always waiting for the next young soul to help.

The water slices against your bow, and the boat's balance feels right as you make your way past the rocky jetty. The open water slaps against the side of the boat as you leave the glassy surface of the harbor behind. You make sail, ensuring all the steps are followed and the teacher's words are upheld. The boat jerks into the soft breeze coming out of the east. You find your bearings on the chart. To be honest, with the amount of studying you've done, you could close your eyes and see the rocky coastline, the islands scattered throughout, and the shallows you're headed to.

The shallows are a collection of sand flats connected by tiny, but surprisingly vast, strips of land. The old shipwright said a great deal of land used to be there, but countless storms blew the sand into the sea and the land was swallowed by the mouth of the ocean. All that remains is a vast space of shallow water two days journey from the port.

You follow the shoreline for some time, keeping it in sight, but the old man warned you not to trust the sea and all the land, for portions of both are waiting to grab at your boat from underneath and tear it apart. The slightest leak was to be treated with immediate attention and fixed. He told stories of great ships that sank due to an unattended leak the size of a pin hole. Old wives' tales you assumed, but nevertheless you would stick to the teaching.

At the third outcropping of rocks, you set your course away from the safety of dry land toward the shallows. As the security of the beach drifts away behind, you try not to look, but after several glances, the shrinking shoreline stirs an emotion in you that is hard to stifle. You try to suppress it by going over your charts and reassuring yourself that the course chosen is true and correct, but after the land disappears from your sight, the nagging fear tugs stronger on your mind.

"Do I have everything I need?" you ask yourself aloud.

The sound of your voice seems to be sucked into the void above the ocean, no reverberation or echo, no solidity to it. This is more disconcerting than the vastness of the ocean itself.

Don't doubt yourself; remember the teachings. You can hear the old shipwright's voice in your head.

You touch your own shoulder for a moment, squeezing like the old shipwright would. Confidence is regained for now, and you continue as the chart outlines.

The sun sweeps across the sky as time passes quickly. Before you know it, the stars begin to take shape as the sun hangs low on the horizon. You dig through your bag for the food you packed: salted fish, bread, and fruit. You think back to a discussion with the old man.

"How much food should I pack?" you ask as he moves to help you shape the planks making up the sides of the boat.

"Does your commission have a timeline on it, days at sea?" he asks without stopping.

You pause to think about it. "No. I don't think so."

"Well, that's good." He continues working as you wait for an explanation, but nothing comes.

"Good how?" you prompt him to continue.

He moves to grab another tool for the job and scratches his head with it. "It's simple. Crystal clear on where to go and what do to, without some thirty-year timeline."

"True, but doesn't that leave it a bit open ended?"

"Sure does." He wipes some dust and sweat from his nose, and he sets the board.

"Can I ask the Harbormaster for clarification?"

"Hold this part here." He pulls your hand over toward the bow. "Obedience is key, but clarification is fine so long as you don't use it as an excuse for not obeying."

"I plan on sailing on time, as long as the boat is ready." You fight not to make eye contact but can't keep the smirk from your face.

"Oh, it'll be ready, but I don't know if its captain will be." He tosses a rag at you, and you catch it.

"But seriously, how much food should I bring?"

The memory brings a smile to your face as you eat a small piece of fish and some bread from your bag. Your commission is rolled out in front of you, the simple words that still hold several questions you read again and again: *REACH OUT TO THE CHILDREN OF THE SHALLOWS.*

Several men in the port gave varying descriptions as to what and who the Children of the Shallows are, some differing so much it is hard to tell the truth from fiction. But the charts don't lie, and you can see that you've made substantial progress toward the shallows. What lies ahead will answer all the questions you've had.

The sunset is beautiful as it comes and goes. The light from the sun encourages, even out on the open water. And with the night comes several other feelings.

The moon stays hidden most of the night and the stars twinkle both against the water and in the sky. The old shipwright's lessons had included going over star charts to follow for navigation, and as you use them, it is clear to see which direction to hold. Sleep pulls at your eyelids, and you nod off from time to time. But when you awaken, you recheck the heading and continue until your eyes cycle closed again.

After several cycles, you awaken to a soft thud and before you in the boat is a man, no older than thirty, wringing the water out of his shirt back into the ocean. You freeze for a moment out of instinct but realize he must know you are there.

"Hello?" you muster.

He puts a finger to his lips. "Shhh." He looks across the surface of the water, eyes locking on a shape in the distance.

You follow his gaze and see the shape moving through the water toward the boat.

The young man sinks down against the bottom of the boat and waits, trying not to breathe.

You watch as the shape sinks further below the surface of the water and disappears into the depths.

"I think it's gone," you say, trying to be casual about it.

He looks up at you. "Are you sure?"

You glance across the surface of the water in all directions around the boat.

"I think," you reply.

"If you don't mind, I'll stay down here a little longer," the man says as he shifts into a more comfortable position. "I'm Charlie."

"Nice to meet you, Charlie." You smirk at the whole situation and what transpired. "How'd you find my boat?"

"Your light," he says, pointing to lantern on the end of the boat. "I was moving around under there when that big guy showed up." He positions his wet shirt behind his head as a pillow.

You grab your bag of food and offer some to him. "What was that?"

He takes a piece of fruit and a smaller piece of bread, taking small bites of both.

"A predator. Ocean is full of them. I thought it was a good night to travel closer to the surface since the moon is hiding, but maybe he figured somebody would be doing that."

He takes his time sitting up all the way, glancing over the edge of the boat at the water's surface until he is convinced nothing is there and continues eating.

"So how is it you pulled yourself out of the water?" you question, thinking about the process you thought to be true and how he circumvented all of it.

"Oh, I've been out of the water before. I needed air, and someplace safe for now."

"When did you first get out?" you ask.

"I was young, many years ago. Pulled from the water, quite a thing," Charlie remembers.

His nervous stomach subsiding, he starts eating larger bites and grabs for another piece of fruit, waiting for your acknowledgement before taking it.

"Go ahead," you say. "If you don't mind me asking, why'd you go back, to the water?"

He thinks on the question as he bites into the fruit, savoring the sweetness of it.

"There were things I had questions about, and it seemed the water was the only place I could find answers. When no one was looking, I jumped in and haven't felt the need to come back out. This time not outstanding."

"Don't you have a family or someone who is looking for you up here?"

"I suppose, but they were busy with other things at the time. So here I am." He checks the water again. "That said, I should be getting on my way. Your sanctuary was much appreciated, and I hope your journey is a safe one." Charlie stands to exit the boat.

"You're welcome on my boat anytime," you add.

Before he slides back into the water, he turns back and asks, "Out of curiosity, where are you headed?"

"The shallows," you say, his face tenses hearing the words.

"Be wary of both the land and sea in the shallows. They shift as much as the people who dwell there. Don't leave your boat for any reason—no matter the request." He waits for your response.

"I, I won't," you say, the words hard to form from the shock of his warning.

"Be well." He waves and slips into the water, disappearing into the depths.

Amazed at the encounter, you play it back in your mind: the predator in the water, Charlie appearing in the boat, the conversation, and the warning. Was Charlie being genuine or was he planting seeds of doubt in your mind like the old man warned you about? You ponder this into the chilly morning hours as you check your coordinates again and slip in and out of sleep.

You awaken to the sun up above the horizon and another bump on the boat, half expecting to see Charlie, but the space he occupied last night is empty. Looking out across the water, you see the boat hit a small sand bar. Pulling the charts out, you find this formation you noticed the day before.

"The crescent bars," you read.

According to the charts, this is the first line of sand bars surrounding the shallows, small openings between the bars allow a boat to pass through, but you must travel around each bar to get to the select openings, and once inside that ring continue to the next and next, like some child's circle maze where the goal is the center.

Not knowing exactly where you hit the outer ring, you decide to travel toward where you think the closest opening may be. You rock your boat off the sand bar, trim your sail, and start along the bar, sailing for what seems like hours with no opening in sight.

You look to the sand bar on your left and question your ability to drag the boat across each of the bars into the center and how much faster that may be. But Charlie's words come back and echo in your head.

Stay in your boat.

You keep your course and eye what looks like a small break in the sand bar up ahead. You cut away from the sand bar to have a better angle at the opening, but as you adjust, you notice your target appears to be moving counter-clockwise.

You follow from a distance, watching the opening move. Not wanting to miss your opportunity, you aim the boat for the opening's anticipated course and slide through as it rolls on behind you. With the first ring passed, it is only a matter of time before you locate the next and the next, navigating each ring and opening as you come to it.

You reach the seventh and final ring and see multiple openings here. You find one and shoot through it. In the middle of all the rings, you set your eyes for the first time on the shallows. The water is flat. If it weren't for a tiny ripple here or there, it looks like glass you could walk on. In the distance, you see something floating in the water. Using your oars, you paddle for the object bobbing up and down.

As you get closer, you realize the object is a person, and several other people bob to the surface nearby. Through the water, you see those below look gaunt and sickly, while those above look fine.

As you approach, one of the people notices you, and in a bit of shock, alerts the others.

"Everyone! A visitor," they say in a welcoming tone.

The floating people stand in the shallows, and those below the surface rise to see the commotion.

A small crowd shuffles its way through the shallows, kicking up the sand and silt. The water becomes murkier the more who join.

"Welcome, welcome!" A tall older man carrying a few extra pounds steps ahead of the rest to welcome you. "My name is Pythios. Who do we owe the honor of this visit?"

"The Harbormaster sent me. It had been a long time since He'd heard word from the shallows," you say as it had been told to you.

"A long time has it been since we've seen the Harbormaster here, but alas there is not much of a harbor anymore." The crowd chuckles in a restrained way, like they had to laugh at Pythios's joke. "And for how long should we expect our most honored guest to stay?"

You stand in silence, unsure what to say. You spent the better part of the journey worried about the journey and never thought about this part of the plan.

You wing it. "I'm not sure, but I'm sure I'll know when it is time to go."

You half wince at the answer, but it seems to appease the crowd.

"Very good. Toss us a bow line so that we may pull you to our small piece of land," Pythios says, nodding to another to go catch it.

You hesitate for a moment, then remember the Harbormaster's encouragement: "Don't be anxious."

You grab the small rope that is attached to the bow and toss it to the man waiting. He takes up the slack and slogs through the water toward a small island.

You make small talk with a few of the people as you go. Pythios stays close, listening to the questions and correcting some of them from the people, anxious about what is being discussed.

As one of the young men is talking, you look ahead to the man pulling your boat and then down at his legs under the water. The water is cloudy from all the movement, but it looks as if his legs are half-rotting away and you can see bone. The silt is too thick to see now, and you excuse yourself for missing the question that was asked of you.

"Do you know a Milly in the harbor, sir?" the young man asks again.

"I don't believe so, but I'm new to the harbor myself. I arrived on another ship a few months ago. Where does she live?"

"I wouldn't know, sir. She left a year or two ago from here, and I haven't seen her since, but I'd love to know she is okay."

"I'll find out when I return and get word back to you." As soon as you speak the words, you want to pull them back. "Or you can come with me?"

The question hangs a moment too long. The young man looks excited at the thought, but seeing this, Pythios jumps in.

"Well, wouldn't that be splendid. I'm sure there will be more time to discuss all of that, but it looks like we are here," Pythios spouts as he ushers the young man to the side and helps pull your boat the rest of the way onto the small shore.

You look at the small, sandy island in the middle of the shallows and the same warning keeps coming back around in your head: *Don't get out of the boat.*

"Now don't be rude," Pythios says as he points to the small gathering on the island. "They're all very interested to hear what you have to say."

"It may be easier for all to hear if I stand at the front of the boat. I'd be higher up there." You sense with each word Pythios's patience wears thin.

Not wanting to offend, you give in.

"I guess for a moment, I could speak on the island."

"Oh good." Pythios reaches out a hand to help you out of the boat, grabbing your arm a little too tight for a friend.

Your foot touches down on the moist sand, not quite dry land, but not the water either. You welcome the ability to stand on a solid space, even though the sand beneath your feet sinks faster than you would think. The man's legs who pulled your boat appear intact now as he pulls the boat up onto the sand.

"This way, this way." Pythios leads you toward the people gathered in a small group toward the center.

You pull the boat a little further onto the sand to be safe and turn to follow him.

The people are a surprisingly diverse group, young and old, well dressed and some hardly dressed. They all have sat themselves down waiting for you to speak. You gather some thoughts and hope your words come out right.

"The Harbormaster sent me. It had been some time since He'd heard from or seen you, and He wanted an account." You look out into the crowd as you speak. Only a few make eye contact, and the other's eyes stare straight into the ground.

Pythios stands to the side, giving you an eye that says, "And?"

"From the tales I've heard, your harbor has long been destroyed, I am more than happy to ferry those who are willing back to the harbor where all are welcome." A few look up, catching your eyes at this offer. You can feel your words working on them. "The trip is easy, and I'm sure there are those in the harbor who'd love to see you."

You find the young man who questioned you earlier. "Milly was it?"

He nods.

"I'll help you find her. The Harbormaster is concerned for your well-being here. For all of you."

Pythios has heard what he needed to make a case. "Why doesn't the Harbormaster return? We are here waiting for Him for years and now He sends you with your tiny boat. We are perfectly fine without a harbor or a Harbormaster for that matter. Do we look like we are in need of anything?"

You scan the crowd and see more needs than you can count: dental, medical, food, fresh water.

"I see people in need of safe harbor, and I will take any who wish to leave."

Water laps up onto the back of your feet, startling you. You move forward and turn to see the ocean has crept up behind you. Pythios stands in the water at his ankles, you see his feet in the water, hardly any skin remains as the water rises.

You turn to see your boat floating in the water away from the ever-disappearing sand island.

"Tides are a tricky thing around here." Pythios beams. "But we have plenty of room for you in our little sanctuary."

You try to remain calm, but don't see an answer to this problem.

"The Harbormaster sought you out. He wants you all there with Him," you shout.

The crowd disperses, defeated by the rising water. They all walk into the depths, their skeletons visible through the clear water. Their hearts are there in the ribcage, but the beat is slow and irregular.

The young man is left on the beach looking at you, then back at the water.

"Come with me." You catch his eyes. "There is nothing left here for you."

He looks back and forth once more then takes off at a run toward your boat, diving into the water and swimming for it as it drifts away.

Pythios grabs your shoulder and tugs you toward the water with him, stronger than you'd think for a man his age.

"You're staying here. The Harbormaster lied to us; He lied to you. Nobody needs a harbor; nobody needs the land. Everything we need is in the water." Pythios spits, his anger boiling over.

You pull yourself away running toward the shrinking edge of shore near your boat. Pythios follows.

"I don't know much, but the water is killing you. Can you not see bones, the flesh rotting away from your own body?"

You push Pythios toward the water, and he falls backward with a large splash.

Pythios stands, considering the water covering his own rotten flesh and looking up at you. "You think we don't know? The choice we've made, that we won't have a Harbormaster dictating our lives anymore. The flesh being removed is freedom."

The young man slides the boat next to you, and you hop in with him.

"No, it is death," you say with a sadness that comes from down deep inside you.

With that, Pythios slides into the deeper water. You set the sail and head away from the middle. The rising tides have covered the maze, and you sail across the water, away from the shallows and the dead that live there.

You sit for a while not knowing what to say. The young man sits, not once looking back to the shallows he came from. You hand him the bag of food, and he eats his fill. After a long while, you break the silence.

"What's your name?"

"Tom," he says while fiddling with a short piece of rope he found in the boat.

"How long were you there?" you pry.

Tom looks across the waves as the boat moves across the water. "My whole life. I remember the harbor, but more like a dream. It had been so long since the last building fell into the water."

"Do you remember what happened? Why the Harbormaster left?" you ask.

"He was gone one day. I don't even remember the day or the time. He may have been gone a week, a month before anyone noticed." Tom stares across the water. "That's when the first people started leaving, once they realized He was gone. Pythios said the Harbormaster would be back and not to worry, but without the Harbormaster's constant shoring up of the jetties, the erosion started wearing away at the shoreline and then the foundations. The docks were battered to pieces in a storm. We were left with what you saw, which Pythios was convinced was all we needed, and after a while, we all believed him."

"The sand around the shallows. It was always moving," you half-ask, half-state the odd fact.

Tom ties several knots in the rope as he speaks, "The shifting sands of the shallows. When the foundation was lost, the sand almost took on a life of its own, always moving. Never letting you feel like you had your footing, always questioning."

"Well, no more of that for you. Solid ground, here we come." You grab a piece of fruit out of the bag and enjoy it.

Tom tugs on the map, pulling it out from under the bag. He looks it over and then at the surrounding waters. "Is this the right heading?"

You glance at the location of the sun and then the map. "We should be fine, from the shallows we needed to head southeast, which we are doing, and that should have us hitting land at some point. The stretch of open water was wide."

"I've never been in water where I can't see the bottom." Tom looks over the edge into the blue depths. "It's a little scary."

You smile. "I'd never seen the surface until I, well, surfaced."

Tom smiles back. "What was it like?"

"It was dark mostly, but when it is all you know, you are used to it. It seems like what life is supposed to be. Until..." You try to form the next part but are lost for words.

"Until you know something better." Tom finishes it for you.

"Exactly," you agree.

Tom looks out across the water. "That doesn't look too good."

Storm clouds are gathering off in the distance starting to consume the sun as it begins its slow journey toward the horizon.

"We should be fine. The man who helped me build this said it could withstand any storm," you say.

Tom thinks on the statement for a moment. "That doesn't seem quite right. Any storm?"

"That's what he said, and I have no reason not to believe him."

A brief time later, the seas are stirred up and the winds blow your small vessel toward your presumed destination.

"What should I do?" Tom asks, needing something to take his mind and stomach off the churning water.

"Try to lash some of this equipment down. The last thing we need is for it to fly around, hitting us," you say as you lean into the rudder to fight the brewing storm.

The waves get larger as the sky darkens and the rain begins. There are several waves surging. They look like great walls of water building up and rolling through the ocean. At times the waves would lift the boat, and it would ride the course until the wave broke or crashed against another wave.

"Keep the water out of the boat as best you can," you direct Tom as you hold the rudder.

It was less the rain and mainly the large amount of water coming from below, splashing into the boat from the waves.

"It is too much!" Tom yells over the crashing waves and the wind.

"No storm too large!" You lock eyes with Tom, a faith in your eyes can be seen.

"What do we do?" Tom cries.

"Tom! Keep the water out of the boat! Focus on that one thing." You meet his eyes and know he heard you this time.

Tom scoops bucket after bucket of water out of the boat, trying not to look at the rest of the storm. You wrestle with the rudder as the waves try to tear it out of your hand.

This continues for what seems like hours, until the waves start calming and the wind dies down. The rain pours, but the worst is over.

Your first storm on the open ocean.

Exhausted, you knock on the Harbormaster's office door.

"Come in, come in," is bellowed from within.

You step inside to see the familiar space.

"You're back! Good, good. Everything go well?" He asks, giving you His attention.

"Only one chose to return with me," you report, not liking the sound of the single number.

"Splendid, that is great. You did great!" He beams at you. "Take some time to rest. We'll talk more soon."

"Thank you, sir." You turn to exit but remember a nagging question and turn back. "Sir?"

"Yes?"

"They said the Harbormaster left them." You don't form a question, but the point is delivered.

He sets his large quill down next to the bit of parchment. "He didn't leave them." He sits back in His large chair. "How did you know I was here?"

You think for a moment, wondering if it is a trick question. "I knocked."

His face is proud as He leans forward again, "Exactly! They stopped knocking a long time ago. They would gather, but not to support the Harbormaster in His work, and that was the beginning of the end for them. The ones who left were smart, but I'm afraid Pythios will never return to a harbor. He sits there afraid of being alone, so he keeps others there with him."

"We could go get them. Send a larger ship. Make them come." You ache to see those people brought back to the safety of the harbor.

Seeing you in this state, the Harbormaster stands and walks around the desk to you, giving you a big hug before pulling back and putting His large hands on your shoulders. He looks you square in the eyes. "Did I commission the captain to send hooks into the deep to rip you from all you knew?"

"No." The depth of His words reaches into you. "I had to make a choice."

"As do they." He says giving your shoulders a squeeze again before returning to His side of the desk and sliding into His chair. "But that doesn't mean we won't do everything we can to try, right?"

"Absolutely, sir. Thank you."

You turn to leave, and the Harbormaster returns to His writing.

There are people in this life who want it both ways: They want the church experience, but they don't want God speaking into their life challenging them. They want the business, but they don't want to sacrifice nights and weekends, endure sixteen-hour days, not take a paycheck the first however many months, or do all the activities that can come with starting a successful business. They want to be healthy, but they don't want the diet and workout routine required to create a healthy lifestyle.

The people in the shallows wanted the harbor, but didn't want a Harbormaster guiding them, helping them maintain it and providing clarity in the harbor's business. While the harbor lasts a while without, decay settles in without a Harbormaster caring for it. The same way a business will fail without proper management and effort, and a healthy body will disappear after dietary and workout discipline does.

All or nothing makes the most sense, yet a halfway life seems to be where many reside. Revelations 3:15-16 says, "I know your deeds, that you are neither cold nor hot. I wish you were either one or the other! So, because you are lukewarm—neither hot nor cold—I am about to spit you out of my mouth."

Bacteria growth is slowed or stopped in the cold, in hot it is killed, but in lukewarm it thrives. It is the same for us. Our passive halfway activities breed poor production and attitudes. But we are the ones who choose our temperature, the same way those in the shallows chose to live halfway between a Harbor and back in the sea, we choose where and how we are going to live.

I challenge you to take an account of which activities you are piping hot, frozen solid, or lukewarm about. Where are you right there in that middle place, phoning it in and giving it the bare minimum effort?

Once you have your list of hot, cold, and lukewarm pursuits, it is time to review. The hot ones you'll identify what makes it so easy to be on fire about it. The cold ones you'll do the same, but considering it is a cold one, it likely isn't taking any of your time on a daily basis. You may find a cold one should actually be a hot one, but you've let it live there because it may be too difficult to tackle currently. Last, the lukewarm ones you need to address why you have chosen to keep it there in middle and if it should become fiery hot or frozen solid.

They are all choices we have to make: the hot, the cold, the lukewarm. That is part of the beautiful life we get to live, God gave us free will to choose, just like those in the Shallows were free to choose. All He asks is that with anything we've chosen we be piping hot about it or completely cold—never in the middle.

CALLED AGAIN

Between the trip and the storm, you were exhausted more than you knew. The tiny hut is a welcome sight as you shuffle up to it after visiting the Harbormaster. He was complicated, but His plan was firm and He didn't waiver. You lie in your bed thinking about what your next commission may be. Sleep takes hold of you, and you drift off.

"Hey." The whisper breaks through your deep sleep.

You try to open an eye, but it is hard to do. The sleep had you. You get a bit of an eye open and see Tom kneeling next to your bed waiting for you to rouse.

"Good morning, Tom." You can't help but include a slight annoyance in your response, but it doesn't faze Tom.

"Morning? More like afternoon. They said you hadn't come out since going in yesterday. I thought I'd better check on you."

"I slept the last twenty-four hours?"

"Yeah, but now you are awake, I got good news!" Tom's genuine excitement was infectious, and you have to bite.

"What?"

"I know where Milly is!" Tom jumps up and then calms himself a bit. "Well, not exactly. I remembered she loves oysters, so I went to the lady in town who sells them and asked her if she remembered a firecracker named Milly who was probably getting them every day. Guess what she said?"

Tom isn't going to let you not play the game.

"She knew her?" you respond.

"Not only that, but Milly worked for her. I mean if you love oysters, why not work at the place that sells oysters, right? Anyway, the lady tells me Milly left on a boat to another harbor to open her own oyster business not too long ago, maybe a year." Tom seems to be done.

"Did you find out the name of the harbor she went to?" you ask.

"Oh, yes." For being so forthcoming, Tom has clammed up, like he knows something else.

"Are you not going to tell?" you pry.

"No... the oyster lady told me something else. I don't know if I agree, but I'm going to try it her way first and see what happens." Tom pauses thinking about the lady's words again. "She said there were other things I needed to do first. She could *feel* it. She told me the name of the harbor, but also said I shouldn't force it. She said I should stick with you, help you, and I'll see Milly again."

"Help with what? It might be months before I get another commission." You sit up, resolved that you aren't going back to sleep.

Before you finish your thought, Tom pulls out a rolled-up piece of paper with the Harbormaster's seal on it.

You look at the paper, then at Tom.

"It was hanging on your door when I knocked," he says as he hands the paper to you.

Now very awake, you kick your legs off the cot and stare at the paper in your hand.

"You going to open it?" Tom asks.

"Yeah," you say, looking thru the rolled-up paper.

Tom makes a face like, "What are you waiting for?"

"Let's go see the old shipwright, a friend of mine." You hop up to change. "Give me two minutes."

Tom obliges, closing the door behind him.

You set the paper on your bed, staring at it as you get dressed. Thoughts race through your mind about what it is and what it means. The negative thought that continues to hound you like a resounding gong in the back of your head seems to be winning out over all the others. You can't seem to shake it as the thought builds a whole narrative in your mind, its own little universe full of cause and effects, consequences and costs.

You finish dressing as the thought solidifies. You snatch up the paper and head out to meet Tom.

You close the door behind you and see Tom nearby kicking a soccer ball around with some kids.

"Tom," you call out and he looks up. He excuses himself from the game.

"We'll play again later." Tom jogs back over to you. "Where we headed, boss?"

"Tom, I'm not your boss," you correct him.

"Okay, okay," Tom says.

"He stays down by the water during the day when he isn't fixing ships; I want to talk to him about this." You hold the paper up.

You and Tom weave your way through the markets and buildings toward the water. Several people along the way stop you to ask about the Shallows and how things went. You give polite answers, introducing Tom to some, but your responses are shorter than needed with each of them, the task at hand overcoming your ability to exhibit the niceties of conversation.

One of the last people to stop you before reaching the water notices the commission paper.

"And another commission so soon?" the woman asks.

"Is that typical?" you ask, testing the waters of the subject.

The woman smiles, her weathered age lines showing a bit. "Nothing is typical when it comes to the Harbormaster's plan, but it does seem quicker than most."

Your gaze drifts over her shoulder to the docks, looking for the old shipwright. She continues talking, but you hear none of it.

"Don't worry though," she finishes, seeing you're someplace else.

"Thank you," you say as you continue toward the docks.

"Were you even listening to her?" Tom asks.

"Of course I was. Why?"

"*Thank you* wasn't a normal response to what she said."

Not wanting to admit your distraction, you lie. "What is normal anymore, Tom? A few days ago, we were in a shifting sands death trap, and today we may be on our way to another one," you say, holding up the paper.

"Maybe," Tom admits.

Up ahead by the docks, you see the old shipwright's chair, empty. You walk up to it, everything seems to be in place, but he isn't there.

You travel along the docks as far as they go. Several ships are loading for their commissions. Large and small the ships prepare for their journeys. Tom can't help himself and has to ask where each vessel is headed. You suppose it is to see if they are going to Milly's harbor.

By the end of the docks, you are starting to show frustration.

"The one person I need right now isn't where I need him to be," you mumble as the thought that took hold earlier builds barricades in your mind, defending itself.

"He'll turn up." Tom's optimism is offensive in the moment.

You return to the old shipwright's empty chair to wait for him, and wait you do. Several hours pass before your level of frustration builds to the point you return to your hut. Tom promises to remain and come get you when the old shipwright returns.

You sit in your hut, staring at the rolled-up piece of paper on the table. A silent battle rages inside your mind. The thought from earlier is well established now, and right thinking is having a hard time destroying the battlements the thought built up over the day.

"Why does it have to be me?" you give voice to the thought that has been plaguing you. "There are hundreds of people in this harbor. I get back, only to be sent again. What about them?"

A loud knock on the door. You jump up to open it. Tom must have found the old shipwright.

As you pull the door open, you don't find Tom, but the Harbormaster standing in front of you.

"Can I come in?" He asks.

"Of, of course." You try not to sound surprised, but this whole thing feels abnormal. The guilt from the thoughts you were mulling over doesn't help the situation.

"I brought us something to drink. This night air is getting colder," He says as He pulls out a flask, setting it on the table. He finds two glasses and sets them by it.

He sits and pours the two glasses, a caramel-colored liquid with a strong odor of apples and cinnamon.

"Sit, sit," He says as He pushes a glass toward you. The glass stops right next to the commission paper on the table. You notice it and see that He does too.

You sit.

"You got the commission? Good. The couriers work hard, but sometimes things get lost in the midst of the day to day." He sips on the drink, noticing you haven't touched yours yet. "Drink up. It's a good brew."

"I haven't opened it yet," you blurt out, trying to come up with some alternate reasoning, not wanting to share the thought built up in your mind.

"I can see that." No judgement, a statement of fact from Him. "Is there a reason why? You seemed so excited a few days ago returning from the last."

"I was... I am. I..." you start in, waiting for a change in His face, looking for disappointment, but finding none, you share the thought. "Why am I being called again? There are people all throughout this harbor who I've heard haven't had a single commission, and I'll have had two."

He sips on His drink, listening to you. As you finish, He smiles and starts, "There are people in this harbor who've never been given a commission like you, yes, but that doesn't mean they don't have a job to do. The overarching commission applies to all, while they wait for a personal commission, they are actively supporting this harbor and its purpose."

You nod like you know what He is going to say as you play with your cup, not having had any of it yet.

"Then you also have people in this harbor who've gotten a commission and declined it," He says frankly.

You look up surprised.

"I don't force it on them," He continues. "Every commission comes with a choice: to go or not to go, to move or to stand still, or worse, to run away."

"How could they ignore it, though? Knowing what we know, what is out there, what they face? How could they forget?" You take a sip of the drink. It is good.

"They don't forget, but they don't think about it. Too caught up in their own lives, they shift focus from their commission to themselves or their kids or jobs or whatever it may be."

He stares into His drink for a moment. "But that doesn't answer your question. Why you? The easiest answer is you have proven yourself faithful, committed. I could use someone else sure, but like you, would you rather have a stranger by your side or, Tom, who by all rights you've only just met, yet even now he sits waiting for the shipwright, committed, for you?"

You look up. The Harbormaster doesn't miss a thing. "You make a good point."

"I've been at this for some time." The Harbormaster finishes the drink and stands to go. "I enjoy these talks. Don't be a stranger. Have a good night."

"Night." You watch as He leaves the small room. Wondering if He has other stops to make tonight.

You finish the drink, mulling over the Harbormaster's thoughts. The last swig moves down your throat, warming you to the core. A peace about the commission comes over you and you crack the seal on the paper, unrolling it, you find the writing inside.

"Wow..." you say as you begin to read.

You don't remember lying down but must have at some point because you sit up fast, awake, and well-rested. Early morning light is peeking through the slats in the hut. No Tom in sight. You wash up, get dressed, and shoot out the door looking for Tom, commission in hand.

On the way to the harbor, a kind, old man cooking eggs hands you an egg burrito and wishes you good luck. At times it feels as though everyone knows more about your commission than you do. You request a second burrito for Tom, and he obliges.

You find Tom where you left him sleeping in the old shipwright's chair. You half want to repay the favor of a startled wake-up with someone right in your face but decide against it. Instead, you touch his shoulder until he stirs.

"Tom, breakfast," you say as his eyes open.

He zeros in on the burrito and is awake and eating.

"Thanks for this." He holds up the nearly finished burrito, devouring it practically whole. "I talked to a few people. They said the shipwright was out repairing a ship on the water, one too big to dock here."

"Well, we will have to get started without him." You hand the opened commission to Tom as he is licking the last flavor of eggs from his hands.

"Oh wow," he says looking it over.

"Why does it have to be me?" This is a question we all face in life. Maybe you phrase it differently: "When do I get a break?" or "When will it be my turn to pick?" My personal favorite I end up saying to myself about once every year is, "What about me? What about what I want?"

I feel like a child the second the words enter my head, and I know where they come from. As a husband I try to hold true to Ephesians 5:25-33, which discusses how a husband should love his wife: "[J]ust as Christ loved the church and gave himself up for her..." Trying to live this out isn't easy. Selfish thoughts creep in, and if unaddressed, like in the story, can grow and eventually harden, making them more difficult to deal with later.

Even as I grow in maturity, I often have to remind myself that every job I'm doing is for God. Colossians 3:23-24 says, "Whatever you do, work at it with all your heart, as working for the Lord, not for human masters, since you know that you will receive an inheritance from the Lord as a reward. It is the Lord Christ you are serving."

In our story, receiving another commission immediately after completing one doesn't seem fair or just—but it may be right. You've been faithful and capable. Recognize the blessing of being entrusted with more. It isn't a punishment. It's a promotion.

You've been chosen because you are ready. You are a proven producer, and in this world that is something to be proud of and celebrate, not complain about.

Keep going! I think you'll find the opportunities will shift and evolve as your capacity increases. With each commission your reach expands, your calling deepens. You may find yourself commissioned to build something bigger than you ever have before. It may be something that scares you, but that is good. That is progress. That is moving forward.

SKELETON CREW

You walk to the docks able to moor galleons and other larger ships. Deciphering the small map on the commission, you come up on a large three-masted galleon.

"This must be the one," you say to Tom.

"*The Return*, that's what she is called right?" Tom asks.

"Yes. *The Return*, first built about thirty years ago, and now we're to take her on a visiting circuit," you say, reading the commission again.

"Visiting circuit?" a voice calls down from aboard the ship.

You look up to see eight people leaning up against railing staring down out at you and Tom. You try to match the woman's voice to the people against the railing, and you have it down to two of them maybe.

"Yes, a series of harbors and villages to visit," you say, hoping you addressed your response to the right person.

"It's a big loop," Tom says, drawing a circle with his finger in the air.

"And you are supposed to do it in this ship?" the woman in the middle speaks, and it matches the voice from before.

"I believe so, if this ship is called *The Return*," you say.

Silence hangs in the air as the group aboard the boat discusses among themselves while you and Tom wait below on the dock.

"Well, come on then," she finally says, waving the two of you up.

Once aboard, you and Tom are face to face with the eight, still not sure what to say as you hadn't read any portion about a crew in the commission and you were so excited to get here with Tom you hadn't put any thought to the need for a crew.

"I'm Carla, and this is the crew of *The Return*," she says introducing the others. "At least what is left of the crew from the last commission she saw. We've been maintaining what we can, waiting for another captain, and you must be it."

You look over the group, both young and old, but they all have the look of sailors. You didn't understand it when the first captain told you about the look of a sailor, but you can see it now in their weathered skin, sun-faded clothes, and steady eyes.

"You can look it over if you need to," you say, offering Carla the commission to review, but she declines.

"I trust you. Of all the ships here, nobody would look at this one twice to steal," she says as the rest of the crew laugh at the notion.

"Any repairs needed before we can depart?" you ask.

Carla and the rest of the crew look at you strangely before all looking up to the yardarms stretched out from the masts, all missing sails.

"*The Return* has sacrificed her own parts to help many ships return to the sea these last few months, and as such is missing several important pieces," Carla says. "Harry here has been keeping a list in case the Harbormaster had a wild idea about her going out again."

Harry walks forward, clipboard in hand. Tom meets him.

"Thank you, Harry. I can gather all the supplies and materials needed," Tom says. "If you all need anything else, just make a list and get it to me."

Carla nods to the rest of the crew who disperse, looking for anything else that hadn't made the list yet.

"Thank you, Carla," you say.

Once the crew is gone, Carla comes closer.

"I hope you realize we will need more crew members," she says.

"Why is that?" you ask.

She stands and looks around at the whole ship and back at you, waiting for you to comprehend something that has gone unspoken.

"This is a galleon. It takes thirty people on a good day to sail and maintain," Carla responds.

"Let me see... crew," you say while looking over the commission again. "Oh, right here... we are to sail with a skeleton crew consisting of Carla, Harry, Bill,

Tony, Chip, Scarlet, Sarah, and Ryan. I know we met Harry, but I take it that is the rest of you."

Carla stands speechless. You're not sure if it is disbelief or admiration in her silence.

You continue to read. "Oh, and we can crew up further on the circuit, but understanding we will need the space for additional passengers."

"A skeleton crew it is," she says, dumbfounded. "I'm going to check on everyone, make sure they are up for it."

"Thank you, Carla!" you call after her.

"This will be fun," Tom says while taking notes on where to get the different supplies on the list.

"Always an adventure," you say.

We imagine a full roster or crew when we picture success. All the roles needed are filled with the exact people you want for the job. There is the number of people we would like to accomplish a job, then there is the number of people needed to accomplish a job. Then there is the bare minimum number of people just to get the job going. That is where the story has you.

You have a dream, a commission, a plan, and what feels like not enough people to do it. Those who are there look at you like you are crazy for thinking you can accomplish this task. Whether it is volunteers at a church, employees at a business, or members of your family, they all want to know where you are taking them, where they are going.

Casting a vision that sticks is critical. Habakkuk 2:2 says, "Then the Lord replied: 'Write down the revelation and make it plain on tablets so that a herald may run with it.'" In other words: Write it plainly. Vision isn't meant to be hidden. As leaders we can know exactly where we are going and how we want to get there but forget to communicate that clearly to the people we need to make it happen. Like those in the story, we receive blank confused stares and don't understand why. We haven't shared the vision clearly and it shows.

A dedicated group of people will follow you for a time, but risk of burnout, decreased productivity, declining job satisfaction, and other issues increase without a clear and decisive vision to fall back on. Your skeleton crew doesn't need to know how it all is going to happen, but they do need you to show them where they are going. This is especially important when you are dealing with volunteers. By the nature of them being volunteers, we assume they already understand the vision and that is why they are there. We take for granted their willingness to serve and assign a role without first casting the vision. As in our story, we charge ahead knowing exactly what we are doing while those around us are lost and don't want to say anything due to our enthusiasm.

Cast the vision and give them the right reason to be on your crew. A crew with a clear vision will sail shorthanded, and sometimes, that's the most faithful way to begin.

THE PEARL DIVERS

The morning air is sweet as you spy the harbor in the distance. The crew, while standoffish for the maiden voyage, has proven quite skilled in the handling of the old ship.

Tony and Chip, brothers—not by birth—have managed to maintain the sails of the galleon, keeping all three trimmed into the wind the entire voyage.

"How are you two so good at that if you'd been drydocked for so long?" you asked early into the journey.

They both just looked at you confused and almost in unison said, "Practice." And went about their work.

You felt foolish at the time. Of course, you didn't have to be out on the water to practice a skill on the water, but you had never thought about doing that. How smart that would be to hone skills in a safe setting. Now with the ship coming up on a new harbor, you are wishing you had put some thought and practice into this first stop.

Your ship, *The Return,* sails into the new harbor. Smaller than your own, the harbor is nestled along a beautiful beach. Several small boats are scattered along the water outside the harbor. They appear to be fishing boats, but nobody is in them.

Out of the water, next to one of the boats, a man surfaces throwing a bag into the boat and pulling himself into it. He waves as you sail past slowly.

"What are they doing?" Tom asks, looking with you at the other boats, where now several others have surfaced, throwing bags and pulling themselves into the boats.

"Scarlet, you know anything about this?" Tony asks as she watches quietly from a capstan, ready to help take in the sails.

Scarlet nods, her eyes fixed not just on the people surfacing, but on the heavy bags that weighed their boats low in the water. She whispers something, soft as can be, and you make out only the word *pearls*. Scarlet has been the most soft-spoken of all the crew thus far but is always deep in thought. You wonder what all was going on in that head of hers, and you look forward to having a conversation at some point.

The ship slowly settles into the dock, and as you and the crew are mooring the ship, several boats approach to greet you.

"Ahoy!" a man hollers to you. "It is always good to see a ship sailing in."

You finish up and disembark to meet the man.

"Morning! What were you doing in the water?" you ask.

The man holds up the bag. You can almost make out what is in it before he tells you.

"Pearl hunting!" he says.

You can now see the bag is full of oysters and mussels. A few other men and women have walked up now, and you can see their bags are full as well.

"I'm Marcus. Come. We'll show you what happens next."

You, Tom, Scarlet, and Tony follow the group as they walk up to a giant open-air shelter with a thatched roof where several others are waiting for them. The rest of the crew stays back prepping the ship to sail again.

Underneath the thatched roof, the group fans out, picking a small piece of ground for each of them and they begin the process of opening their catch, looking for pearls.

Tom, having acquired a taste for oysters, hovers around, curious, rubbing his stomach, and wondering what they will be doing with the meat.

Tony wanders the room, looking over what is in each bag and the size of each person's catch.

Scarlet makes her way to the middle of the room, as if knowing what she would find there. She stares sadly, but you can't see at what as Marcus ushers you to sit with him.

You sit, watching as Marcus carefully slips his knife between the shells and pries the oyster open, revealing the creature within. He feels for a pearl within and finding none, discards the shell and creature to the side.

"Do you not eat them?" you ask.

"No," Marcus replies without looking up, absorbed in the task. "Just need the pearl."

You look around. Unlike the lively chatter of a fish market, there is only silence and intense focus on the singular task.

"A pearl!" someone shouts across the room.

Everyone looks up, some with grimaces, at the person who spoke up.

She holds the pearl high as she walks toward Scarlet and a shrine at the middle of the space you couldn't see before now. Several people follow her, while others wave hands in disregard. Curious, you rise to see what she is doing.

As you approach, you see the shrine is made of driftwood, crowned by an enormous pearl nestled inside an oyster shell.

The young woman clutches her pearl tightly as she approaches the shrine. She opens her hand next to the massive pearl, resting it there.

It is obvious her pearl is smaller, and those who followed her up there let her know it. Laughing at the smaller size of her pearl compared to the one sitting there, they turn back to their own catches, eyes searching for pearls worthy of the shrine.

"Yours is a beautiful pearl," Scarlet attempts to comfort her.

"Not good enough," she sighs, tossing the pearl into the driftwood shrine where it hits several branches before settling on top of a pile of many other pearls that didn't make the cut. She walks back to her bag, resuming the activity.

Before long, all the bags lie empty, shells and debris scattered across the ground. Small crabs, aware of the ritual, scuttle toward the discarded oyster and mussel meat, feasting on the remnants Tom didn't get to.

The group gathers their bags, and with heads hanging low, they start back for the boats.

"Wait. You are going again?" you ask Marcus.

He turns back to you, looking defeated.

"They have to," Scarlet says, answering for him. "They have to measure up to that pearl's standard."

Marcus nods.

"This is what we do," he says.

"Where is the Harbormaster?" you ask.

Marcus shrugs and starts walking with the group back down to the docks.

"Marcus, wait up," you say.

You and Scarlet spend the rest of the day with Marcus, learning the harbor's history and the origins of the pearl shrine. Scarlet listens quietly, and you struggle to understand the hold the comparison ritual has on everyone and how it could have gone on for so long.

"All harbors have this sort of thing," Marcus says.

"No they don't. I haven't been to many, but I've never seen or heard of anything like this," you reply.

"It is more than you may think," quiet Scarlet says. "Some use pearls, others trinkets and gold coins, homemade crowns that grow and grow until they are so large the people would fall over."

"Really?" you ask.

"Really," Scarlet says, "But it is all pointless, Marcus. Where I grew up it was the same way. Always trying to measure up. It all starts as beauty and becomes an impossible burden."

Marcus mulls it over for a moment.

"Then how do we know if we've earned it?" Marcus asks.

"Earned what?" you say.

"This." Marcus points all around him. "This life. How do we know we deserve it?"

"We don't," Scarlet responds. "We never earned it. It's a gift that is offered to everyone. But we did have to accept it. You remember that, right?"

"I don't know. Yeah, I guess, but it seems too easy," Marcus says.

"Far from it," a newcomer says, walking up from the water.

You all look up seeing who this intruder is.

"Charlie!" you and Marcus say in unison.

You are beyond surprised to see the man who climbed into your boat in the middle of the night on your way to the shallows.

"What are you doing here?" you ask.

"I'm here all the time. What brings you here?" Charlie says as he greets Marcus.

"Another commission—making the rounds with this crew. This is Scarlet," you say, introducing her. "First stop here, then on to several others Harbormaster wanted us to check on."

"As He does," Charlie says. "The cost is great Marcus..."

Tom and Tony wander up to see who the newcomer is.

"Tom, this is Charlie, the one I told you about in the middle of the ocean when I was sailing to you," you say.

"No kidding?" Tom replies. "I thought that was all made up when you told me some random guy pulled himself into the boat in the middle of the ocean. Nice to meet you!"

Charlie drifts off in thought as he sees someone further down the beach.

"Sorry, guys, I have to go see someone," Charlie says. "It was nice to meet you. If you're still here when I get back, we'll talk more."

Charlie walks alone down the beach. Far off, a lone figure—perhaps the Harbormaster, though the distance obscures certainty—stands waiting for him.

You and Scarlet spend a little more time with Marcus. Scarlet shares her upbringing and the "pearls" that consumed her family's life. All the things she was taught to believe about needing the pearls and how she finally broke free from living that way.

"Trust me, you don't need the pearls," Scarlet says, as you, Scarlet, Tom, and Tony join the rest of the crew back onboard the ship to leave.

"We'll consider it," Marcus says, waving goodbye as you pull out of the harbor.

"Think they'll listen?" Scarlet asks as you steer the ship onto the next destination.

"I don't know," you say. "But I hope they do. Thank you for sharing the way you did. I know that can't be easy, having to relive some of those experiences."

"You're welcome," a gentle smile on her face as she replies. "We live our lives wondering how any of the junk we lived through will benefit us later on, and then I get a day like today and it reminds me."

"What's that?" You ask.

"I didn't go through that for me. I went through that so I could share with Marcus and anyone else who needs to hear the truth about pearls."

"Amen." Tony and Chip say in unison.

You and Scarlet turn, not realizing, they, and the rest of the crew, were listening in. You all laugh.

"On to the next?" you ask everyone.

"Aye, aye!" they say.

The comparison game is one you can never win. There will always be someone better or worse—never the best.

The story tackles something many of us may have issues with. Historically, you had a smaller window into the world with which to compare, but social media has opened that window up wide and is now a notorious vehicle of the comparison game. You can see at any waking moment the presented state of other's lives. Their "pearls" are on full display for all to see, at least the side of the pearls they want you to see. We forget what is placed on social media is curated and only the best things make it there. The best pictures, the best vacations, the best moments.

I think we'd all agree we shouldn't play this game, but it is too easy to fall back into the patterns of comparison. In our story, the divers found a purpose in the comparison, so they work and toil to find pearls that measure up to this glorious one, but the problem is they can't find one, they always come up short. As Christians, we often put a large pearl on display—rules and standards we claim as markers of holiness. But that pearl is not a treasure—it's a shackle and chain. We lift the pearl as something to aspire to, all while it weighs us down and keeps others away. Worse yet are the unspoken pearls: how someone dresses, what they drink, if they have tattoos, if they use the "right" church words. These pearls don't reflect the Kingdom. They just reflect us trying to measure righteousness in human terms.

We'll discuss later the value of measurement when it comes to our plans and projects, but there is no place for this comparative measurement game. There is no measuring tape you can use or thing you can do that will help you measure up to God's standards. Romans 3:23 says, "[F]or all have sinned and fall short of the glory of God."

God doesn't ask us to fit in any size outfit or to say eighty-thousand prayers before our forty-second birthday or anything like that. He sent Jesus for us exactly as we are, sin and all, an offering for all of us, a gift. All we have to do is accept it. We must stop trying to measure and compare. The things we have been called to do are much too important to waste time with that game. What pearls are you holding onto? Set them aside and get on with the mission.

If you declare with your mouth, "Jesus is Lord," and believe in your heart that God raised him from the dead, you will be saved."
Romans 10:9

THE DESERTED ISLES

The water slaps against the bow as the ship cuts across the strait between harbors.

"We are to resupply at the deserted isles," Tom says, confused as he reads the orders.

"If they are deserted, how are we going to resupply?" you ask.

"According to Harry, they aren't really deserted. You remember sailing around sandy point? Which was actually all rocks, not a grain of sand in sight," Bill, the ship's navigator, answers as he looks over the map in the captain's quarters.

"Then why the name? Was it deserted at one point?" Tom asks.

Bill looks at you and Tom and back at the maps and pages of several books, looking for an answer. "It says here that the name comes from the fact that people leave the isles soon after arriving. They desert them. Nobody stays there that long."

"What about the people who live there?" you ask.

Bill pushes the book over to you. The pages are blackened in places, and the only legible words are what he already read.

"But Harry said there are people there?" you ask trying to ensure the trip is not in vain.

Tom exhales, shoves back from the big map table, and strides toward the door, opening it and gazing out, looking for good ole Harry.

"Harry! Can we have a word about our destination?" Tom hollers across the deck.

"Aye!" is heard over the sound of the ocean.

A few moments later, Harry hurries through the door. Harry is a beast of a man. Though built like a wall, Harry moves with the humility of a man who knows the damage he could cause and chooses not to.

"Yes, Captain. The deserted isles," he says, looking to you for further guidance.

"Are there people there?" you ask.

"Aye, there are... people there." The pause apparent in his response.

"What about them, Harry?" Bill presses.

Harry considers his next words, trying to sum up past hurts as simply as possible.

"I was born there. People say I don't talk much, but I used to. The isles are deserted by newcomers because they can't deal with the talking."

You and Tom look at each other, confused.

"Talking? The people talk a lot?" Tom asks.

"They don't listen, and worse—whatever comes to their minds, they say it. Most of it brimming with hate and judgment. If you're born into it, you know nothing else, but no visitor stays. Nobody."

Tom looks at Harry, then to you. Bill sits silently, more comfortable with his maps and charts.

"Sounds cozy." Tom's timing with his humor still lacks a certain tact.

"Thank you, Harry," you say, "When we arrive, I want you to help... navigate communicating with them."

"Aye, Captain," Harry says as he turns and heads out of the captain's quarters.

You turn to Tom and Bill. "That doesn't sound like fun. Is there anywhere else to resupply?"

"There is, but the orders are clear: this is the place," Tom says, looking to Bill for confirmation.

Bill nods in agreement.

You look over the map again at several other locations but are drawn back to the deserted isles. The map looks the same all over, but now knowing what you do, there seems to be a shadow cast over the three small blips of land on the paper. You sigh, knowing what must be done.

You push the map back over to Bill. "Plot the coordinates then, let's hope they are happy to see Harry."

Despite the grim warning, you aren't prepared for how sunny and sandy the isles appear. The buildings up from the shore look well-kept and several people wave as you cut across to the large port.

The port itself isn't desolate, but whether from new construction or lack of use, everything appeared quite... clean.

"Where would you recommend, Harry?" you ask.

Harry thinks for a moment. "Far Dock will be easier to load and allow us to depart quicker toward our next destination."

"Make it so, Tom," you say.

Tom jumps into action as the first mate calling out each crewmember by name.

"Tony and Chip. Let's get the main sails shaped and stowed, take us in on the aft sail. Harry, prepare to moor the bow. Carla, prepare to moor the aft. Scarlet, help with the sails. Sarah, stow the ropes. Ryan, start bringing up the empty crates for resupply. Bill, to the crow's nest, if you please."

As everyone else sets about their work, Bill eyes you and then Tom, lets his shoulders fall, then begins the climb up the main sail to the nest.

"You know he isn't a fan of heights," you whisper to Tom.

"Only Tony and Chip are in this crew, and they have the sails," Tom replies. "They're all going to have to get used to doing each job with such a small crew."

You walk to join Harry at the front of the ship while he waits to rope the cleat nearest the bow to bring the ship to a stop.

"How we doing, Harry?" you ask.

"I'm fine overall, one benefit of having grown up here. When I left, I said my piece and left it all on the table. For better or worse."

Harry ropes the cleat and secures the long line.

A small group begins to gather on the docks, watching the boat settle into its spot. A few of the younger men come over and offer to help with the ropes.

Harry eyes them, waiting for some remark about how they can't even dock the boat themselves, even though they were fine, but nothing ever comes.

You thank them for their help, and they nod in return.

A small man with thick-rimmed glasses, a small tuft of black hair on his head, and a large smile with only a few teeth left walks up to you and Harry. Ignoring you for the most part, he stares at Harry. All of the sudden recognition breaks through, and the smile gets that much bigger.

"Harry! Is that you?"

"Aye, Herman. It's me," Harry replies.

"You're all grown up! Such a blessing to see you return, even if only for short time. I'm sure your family will be pleased to see you. Should I send someone for them?" Herman says with what appears to be genuine sincerity.

An awkward silence hangs as neither Harry nor you know how to navigate this unforeseen circumstance.

"We'd love to resupply, if possible." Tom breaks the silence, trying to get his job done. "This is the list of things we need, most important things at the top. At the bottom are a few items we'd love to have but can make do without."

"Of course, of course... a mission to tend to," Herman says with what feels like a twinge of sadness, taking the list from Tom's outstretched hand and reviewing the items. "Shouldn't be a problem for most. If you can wait a single day, I can have everything here before the sun sets tomorrow."

He looks to you then to Harry and finally to Tom for an answer.

"That'll be great," you respond, still waiting for the biting comment or backhanded remark, but none comes. "And thank you." You try to remember your manners.

Herman begins directing his people to gather the supplies needed. You listen, waiting for the things Harry had told you about in their speech. Looking to Harry, you can see the confusion on his face as well.

"That's not what I said, you worthless...!" Somewhere deeper in the crowd, you hear the words that ring truer to what Harry had told you about, but they never finish. Instead, a softer voice can be heard defusing whatever disagreement had taken place.

"You're frustrated, you feel misheard, but we are better than that. We are patient, we are kind," the voice finishes.

Almost in unison, the small crowd speaks together, "We are patient, we are kind."

Herman sees the confusion on Harry's face.

"A lot has changed, my boy." Herman thinks for a moment. "Please allow me to fetch your parents. You have no idea how upset they'll be if they don't get to see you. They moved out of town, so it'll already take them a bit to arrive if I send someone now."

Harry turns to you. "Captain, with your permission, I'd like to go see them myself if it's possible."

You look to Tom, and he nods in agreement.

"Absolutely, Harry. By Herman's account, we won't be fully supplied till tomorrow afternoon. Check back by then."

Herman calls out for one of his helpers, "Christopher!"

A young man appears out of the group of people working. He shares several of Harry's features, is much younger, but undoubtably is family.

"Christopher, can you show your cousin here the way to his parent's house?"

Christopher brightens up. "Are you Harry? Oh! I've heard so much about you! Well, you know from before you left. I was too young to remember it really. Tell me about the ocean, the world. Where have you been? What have you done?"

Harry starts walking with the young man, looking back and smiling, something you hadn't known him to do much in your time with him.

"He doesn't recognize the place," Herman says, eyes tracking Harry with a soft smile.

"What happened here? This wasn't how it was described to me at all."

Herman thinks for a moment. "You have some time. It'll help if I can show you."

Herman begins walking before you've agreed, but you walk ahead with him out of curiosity.

The stroll through the town is pleasant, and Herman describes some of the history of the place, the construction of the buildings, all very light topics, but upon reaching an old wooden fence, he becomes somber and ushers you in.

"It's a short way ahead. Follow the trail; you'll find the marker easy enough. I'll be here when you return."

You pause, looking up the path and back to Herman who holds out a hand pointing down the path. You nod in understanding and walk up the path as directed. The trail winds up and around several beautiful overlook points on the ocean below. You pass an elderly couple on their way down, the wife crying, and the husband—with his arm around her shoulder—nodding to you as you pass, as if he is exchanging some sort of knowing recognition in your travel.

The path winds around one more time to reveal the end: an overlook where a large stone marker sits to the side. Two small trees have been planted on either side of the stone. Strips of fabric and yarns are tied to their branches. You walk up to the stone and see the words carved into it; they break your heart.

The jump onto the rocks below did not cause the greatest harm. It was our words that cut deepest those we loved. They sought the rocks that shatter bones and spill blood to find relief from our words. What then shall we do. We must be patient. We must be kind. We must.

You stare at the words on the rock, then look around it at the overlook point, moving toward the edge where a small wooden fence has been erected. Scattered on the rocks far below, some covered by the water and the waves, is the bleach white color of bones, thousands, hundreds of thousands. The remnants of the people who couldn't do it anymore and wanted out.

At some point, tears creep into your eyes and slip down your face as the overwhelming pain and hurt of these lost souls weighs on you. You spend several moments in silence thinking over your own words and the things you've said in the past that could've cut a person in that way. You start to catalog the things that went unsaid, when you know you had the opportunity to uplift but chose not to for one reason or another, too busy to notice, too prideful to admit.

You read the rock again on your way out. "We must be patient. We must be kind... I must be patient; I must be kind."

Herman is waiting for you as he promised. He begins the walk back to town. Without speaking, you follow.

"When did it all change?" you ask, breaking the silence between you.

Herman stops, bending down to look at a small patch of flowers growing along the path.

"We'd always had people who chose that... path," he says.

Herman admires the flowers, watching a bee crawl over them.

"After, we'd call them weak, cowards for taking that way out."

Herman watches as the bee moves on, carrying pollen back to its hive.

"A few years after Harry left, we held our usual townhall meeting. Voices rose. People Shouted. And that night, sixty-seven people walked the path. None walked back down."

Herman strokes the petals of one of the flowers, a small purple and yellow one.

"I'm sorry," you say, watching him look at the flower.

"That was the beginning, but it still took a while for it to take hold of everyone. Several people found it easier to blame the path being treacherous, or the darkness. They tripped and fell, they said. Any reason was easier to stomach than the one written on that stone. We took what we thought was our greatest strength in hand, speaking truth, and shined the light back on ourselves, and it was ugly. Still is ugly. None of it happened overnight, and our weekly townhall meetings can still get a little loud, but it comes from a different place. That is what has changed the most. The place our words come from."

Herman leaves the pretty little flower be and stands again.

"I'd imagine that was hard, changing everything you'd believed and done prior to that," you say as Herman looks on.

Hearing the words, he turns back to you, a sorrow in his eyes.

"I'd have changed a lifetime ago if I knew the pain I was causing by speaking. I'd have never spoken another word if I knew... the permanent damage."

You realize where his depression is coming from.

"Who was it?" you ask.

"My wife..." he chokes out. "My youngest son and his wife, one of my apprentices from the docks. Several others I considered friends, but I never treated them as such, not really, knowing what I know now."

He looks over the picturesque landscape as the sun begins to settle toward the horizon. Then he looks at you, deep into your soul, grabbing your shoulder with one hand.

"It's never too late to make things right. For you, for me, I try to be better for them. They deserved better, and I want to die someday knowing that every day since I lost them, I tried to live a life that would honor their memory."

And with that, he releases your shoulder and ushers you down the path back to the ship to check the progress.

You offer to take Tom and the rest of crew to visit the stone marker the next morning. You warn them all of what is at the end of the trail, giving opportunity to stay back should they not want to go. Everyone goes, but Sarah hangs back before the marker, not wanting to approach. She takes a moment there herself and walks back down the hill singing a slow sad melody.

You and the rest of the crew slowly make your way back down the hill. Carla walks alongside you and Tom, watching Sarah far up ahead.

"Sarah's brother," she starts, words catching in her throat. You wait for more but realize that it isn't going to come. It is too hard.

"I understand," you say.

Carla nods and jogs ahead to walk with Sarah.

"Tom, I know I can be harsh at times and stubborn, but I want you to know how thankful I am for you," you say as you and Tom are walking back to the ship.

"Oh, I know," Tom replies.

"But I've never said that, and I want you to know I am," you say.

Tom thinks on it a moment. "I appreciate you saying it, but I do know. You've shown me a hundred different ways over the short time we've spent together. And if I had to choose between hearing it or seeing it, I'd take seeing it—every time."

You think on a reply, but then let it be, feeling even more thankful for the first mate Tom has been.

The ship was resupplied on time as Herman had promised.

"Thank you, Herman," you say, shaking his hand, "We'll make sure your harbor is included on the routes regularly again. We'll let them all know how far you've come."

Herman nods in thanks, teary-eyed he hugs you.

"Herman you've gotten soft in your old age," Harry says walking up with who can only be his family following close behind.

"I have... Thankfully, I have Harry. Harbormaster knows we needed it," Herman says. Harry grabs Herman to hug him.

"Thank you, Herman. I'm sorry for everything you had to endure, but thank you for the leader you are here. The example you are," Harry chokes out.

Harry lets the man out of his huge hug, and Herman nods to everyone once more before walking back to his office at the docks.

"I'm glad you made it back Harry," you say.

"About that, Captain," Harry says looking back to his family and back to you, "I'd like your permission to stay here for a bit. I talked to the Harbormaster. He said he would love for me to stay, but said I should make sure it was okay with you."

Your mind reels. *The Harbormaster wanted him to ask if it was okay with me?*

"Who am I to disagree, Harry?" you say. "We'll miss you, but I can't tell you how happy it makes me to know this mission brought you back to your family."

"I'll watch for your sails, and if you'll have me, I'd crew with all of you again," Harry says.

"You're welcome on my ship anytime, Harry," you say shaking his hand.

The crew takes a moment to say goodbye to their friend. They spent years on a drydocked ship together. You decide to give them all the minutes they needed to say farewell.

As *The Return* slips free of the dock, you and your crew watch Harry wave with his family. His big smile lifts you up and puts wind in each of your sails. You lift your hand, waving farewell, and sail away with a heart more hopeful and a mouth more careful than when you'd arrived.

Let us be more patient, let us be more kind—today, tomorrow, always.

Our words matter. The power of our words is *not based on our own perception* of the words, but by how those words have been received by the people they were directed at. In our story we had a group, who, in their minds, were the most honest and direct of people—character traits that in and of themselves aren't bad. But without considering the weight of their words on the people receiving them and the spirit in which the words were spoken, they left a trail of destruction with their mouths.

The Bible touches on this in several places. In Proverbs 12:18 we find, "The words of the reckless pierce like swords, but the tongue of the wise brings healing."

If we could see in real time the damage our words cause to others, the sword thrusts as we speak and the resulting wounds, the bleeding because of it, I think we would take more care with our words. Very few of us would strike another person in anger with our fists, but we'll stab them through the heart with a sentence or two.

In First Corinthians 13 it starts with a list of great abilities but quickly lets us know that without love those abilities are pointless. We then learn the two things that love is in verse four, "Love is patient, love is kind."

Take account of your words, what you say and why you say it. Are you speaking to build and heal or speaking to pull down and destroy? If it is the latter, I promise you it is better not to speak at all. Let your words build with love. Let your words heal with love. In order to truly show love: We must be patient. We must be kind. We must.

Anchors Aweigh

The ship drifts with the current, tugged this way and that by the wind and waves. Chip and Tony wrestle the final sail down, working in practiced sync despite the chaos. The rest of the crew struggles to make their repairs and see that the ship stays above the water.

Carla and Ryan crank either side of the bilge wheel, each gripping a handle. With each rotation, the manual bilge pump strains, sucking water from the lower hold out of the boat and over the side.

Several holes riddle the underbelly of the ship, but the two largest holes, put there by rocks unseen below the waterline, allow the same amount of water in as is being pumped out. Sarah and Scarlet work quickly to hammer plugs of wood and canvas into the gaps to quell the rush of water, but it appears the battle is being lost.

Upon leaving the deserted isles, a small storm pushed the ship off course into shallow water.

"Captain! We aren't making any progress; we have to anchor," Tom hollers up from below.

You hear the heavy concern in Tom's voice. Knowing the negative potential outcomes of anchoring you make a decision.

"Lower the port anchor, Har...!" you say, catching yourself. "The port anchor, Bill."

Bill hesitates—then nods in understanding—it hadn't been long at all since that was Harry's job, and this was just another unfortunate reminder that everyone's friend wasn't on the ship anymore.

You watch as Bill rushes toward the front of the boat, throwing a lever with a quickness. The large anchor releases and falls—disappearing into the water below—the chain clatters behind it followed by the long coil of heavy rope. Moments later, the line snaps taut as the anchor slams against the ocean floor and secures itself.

The crew pauses, feeling below and observing the ship's placement above to determine if it is still moving. The current and wind both playing a part pulling at the ship and ultimately the anchor. Despite the anchor's grip, the ship drifts further with the wind, and the crew recognizes it.

"Captain, permission to drop the second anchor?" Bill asks.

You weigh the decision. A second anchor might hold—but if the seabed is rocky, retrieving both anchors could prove difficult, especially without Harry's strength cranking the large wooden capstan used to haul the anchors up.

A rogue wave pushes the ship, spinning it sharply on the single anchor. The deck tilts—listing hard to port. Chip—caught off guard—reaches with nervous hands grabbing a second rope above, legs dangling for a moment before he regains his footing.

"Drop the anchor." You give the order.

Bill hurries forward but slides as the ship begins to list further over. He dives and flips the other lever and releases it—the rope hissing through the pulley before catching with a jolt. The ship settles in place still leaning badly.

A wave of relief ripples through the crew. Chip and Tony fist-bump. Carla and Ryan high-five. Even Bill lets out a breath of relief. The ship is holding.

With the ship secured, you finally turn your whole attention inward—helping the crew repair what's been damaged, helping right the ship.

"How's it coming?" you say as you wade into the water that has filled the hull.

Tom, Chip, and Tony haul buckets of seawater from the hull—speeding up the process the pump began.

"Holding just under five feet it looks like now," Tom says handing a bucket off to Chip to carry up and hand off to Tony to dump over the side.

"Good work everyone! Especially you ladies," you say.

Sarah and Scarlet—drenched from head to toe—have obviously been working underwater on several of the holes.

"Where do you need me?" you ask.

"How big are your hands?" Sarah asks, already pulling a piece of canvas.

You show her—palms wide. She nods and wraps them with expert speed.

"That'll work," she says.

Sarah guides your hands to two holes in the hull beneath the water.

"We ran out of plugs that size, and the water keeps pushing the canvas out," Scarlet says.

"Whatever you need," you say as you stand awkwardly, stretched out with two hands plugging holes—the water occasionally splashing your face as they work around you.

"I'd never ask you to do this if we weren't anchored," Sarah says as the water line slowly starts falling.

"Why's that?" you ask.

"Too much movement. Even with the canvas, it'd wreck your hands," Sarah says.

"I'm glad I put that second anchor down then," you say.

Sarah makes an unsure face.

"What?" you ask.

"Anchors are tricky things, without Harry to help break them free from the ocean's floor..." Sarah drifts off in thought.

"I thought about it, but knew we had to steady the ship. We'll get the anchors up Sarah," you try to assure.

"Thankfully we just have the two," she says.

"How many do other ships have?" you ask.

"How many should they have? One or two sized for the ship," Sarah says as the water starts to dip below one of your hands. She pulls your hand out and Scarlet gives her a freshly carved wood plug to take its place.

Sarah drives the plug into place with a large mallet sealing off the hole.

"I saw a ship with four once, each weighing 8,400 pounds," she says wiping the water away from the hole to check for any still seeping through. None comes.

"Ship wasn't even that big, but they sure loved their anchors," she says. "Almost more than their ship."

"Did they ever use them?" you ask.

"Once they put those heavy things down, I don't think they ever got them back up. Safer to stay stuck than to risk sailing," she says.

"We'll get our anchors up," you say.

"I'm sure we will, Captain," she says, smiling sincerely.

It is slow work, but the water is pumped out, the rest of the holes are plugged, and the ship sits straight once again.

The sun comes out, and everyone takes a few moments to let it warm the skin and dry off the clothes.

"I know we're all tired, but we need to weigh anchor. We need to get moving again," you say, catching Sarah's appreciative glance.

The crew doesn't complain. They all stand and move first to the aft capstan.

It takes everyone to haul the anchors back up, each crew member straining as the chains groan and the capstan creaks. But link by link the chains rise and the anchors behind them—emerging from the deep, caked in sand and seaweed—break free. The anchors ascend back into their resting place.

"Anchors aweigh, Captain," Sarah says as she turns her eyes to the horizon, ready for whatever comes next.

The ship gets underway. Standing at the wheel, you ponder the anchors—how easy it would've been to rest in the sun, repair additional damage, both anchors holding firm. But that isn't the mission. That's not your purpose.

The anchor plays a pivotal role in the function of the ship. As in our story, movement must be halted at times, and the anchor is just the tool to do it. The complex thing about "anchors" in our lives is that they show up in many different forms. Some are helpful, but if left too long, they can become detrimental to progress—they keep us stuck. In Luke 14:26, Jesus speaks about the cost of discipleship—calling us to love Him more than even family. The "roots" we put down in life can act as anchors, hold us in place when we're called to move.

When our orders change and a new calling arises, we should be ready to move. The more anchors we've put out make it difficult to be agile. You must lift them to set your course, but at times we've allowed them to become too heavy for us move alone.

In America, debt is a large anchor. Debt requires the individual to maintain a certain level of income to repay the debt, which means steady employment. Debt becomes a tether, one link after another forming the chain of a big anchor. Family can act as an anchor as well, both in good and bad ways. The stability a strong family brings during life's storms is a blessing. But when you feel called to move will the same family be okay with weighing anchor. We are forced to consider several additional factors when there is family involved. If the Lord sends you to the inner city of Chicago, the rural countryside of Alabama, the favelas of Rio de Janeiro, or a forgotten tribe in the Philippines, the needs of the family play a critical part in the decision. We may begin to tell God this calling should wait for a better time because we have convinced ourselves that we must consider all the ways it will affect our family before we step out in faith.

Now is the time to identify some anchors. So, take inventory. What anchors are in your life right now? You may have received your orders already or are anxiously waiting for them, but if you were asked in this moment to step out in faith, what would keep you from saying, YES?

I know the easy answer is family or finances, but those are just two of many reasons we may have why we don't move. My brother, sister-in-law, and *four* kids lived in the jungle on an island in the South Pacific. That was their calling, and they answered. Was it easy? Absolutely not. Answering a call like that takes time, sacrifice, and a heart prepared to obey. What are those things anchoring you? What is keeping you from answering the call?

Begin lifting the anchors, get more hands on the capstan if needed, and slowly start raising them off the seafloor so you can get underway and on to what God has for you.

Don't Burn the Ships

The small island village was founded by these people not because of its great location or access to water, food, and supplies, but out of necessity. The founders were adrift for several weeks when they happened upon this place. It wasn't large, but it had trees and solid ground—enough to make repairs to their ship. As the work progressed, the members of the crew not working on the ship spent their days exploring the island and found an extensive cave system. It was as if the island kept revealing more of itself to them over time, and they fell in love with the idea of it.

"What if we stayed here?" someone said. "What if we make this our home? What if we build some buildings to help with the process of repairing?"

So they did, and piece by piece, parts of their ship were used toward the construction of buildings. Finally, after much debate, they decided to break down the ship to better make this place a home. They didn't burn it in a bold declaration of moving forward. They simply stopped. The mission they had set out on faded away, and they were left living on the island. It was a content life. Some would call it rich and full, but it also left some of them asking the question as they lay in their beds on their way to sleep, "What if...?"

Their commission remained unfulfilled—and they knew that couldn't be good in the grand scheme. They settled in this place because they were tired, troubled by storms with too much wind and doldrums with too little. But they did choose this new life, still believing in the purpose of the life before, still believing in the Harbormaster's plans, but now cheering from the shore—no longer on the water.

"The Harbormaster hasn't forgotten your commission," you say, "He asked us to stop here—not in judgment—but to remind you that the work is still unfinished. If you're willing to pick it up again, we'll gladly take you on."

The village's leader listens to your words and thinks.

"If you choose to stay here, He understands and won't be a bother," you say. "But He did ask you keep in touch."

"I'm sure He would join you too," Ryan adds. "If invited."

"Always," you say with a nod to Ryan.

"We'll have to discuss it," the village leader says. "Please wait here, and we'll let you know our decision."

"Of course," you say.

The group of village representatives walk down the small dock away from the ship.

"Think they'll stay?" Carla asks.

"I would," Bill says, to the shock of everyone else. "I mean if I was them. Look at this place."

Everyone looks over the village and surrounding area.

"It is beautiful," Scarlet says. "But not where they are supposed to be."

"I wasn't where I was supposed to be," Tom says, walking over next to you, "until the Harbormaster sent this guy in the tiniest boat you've ever seen to come get me."

Everyone smiles at the thought.

"It wasn't that small," you say, defending your first vessel.

"That boat was so tiny," Tom says, waiting a beat.

Carla, picking up on it, responds, "How tiny was it?"

"It was so tiny our mast doubled as a fishing rod," Tom laughs, amused at himself.

Everyone either laughs or shakes their head in embarrassment at Tom's humor.

"I don't get it," Bill says, leading to another wave of laughter.

"Tom, while we wait, can you and Sarah take a look at those hull repairs using the supplies they gave us?" you say, smiling.

"I'll help," Scarlet offers, jumping up from her seat on the bridge steps.

"We'll get her put back together, Captain," Sarah says.

"Bigger," Tom says, letting it hang, "and better than ever."

The three disappear below deck carrying boards and tar the villagers provided upon request when you docked.

Tony and Chip stand at the railing waiting.

"How long do you think they'll take?" Tony asks.

"They've been here a while," Carla says, thinking. "I'd imagine it may take them a while. At least the day."

Chip looks to Tony, and in their silent way of communicating, they agree to a game of cards and set off toward the bow to find a couple crates to use as a table. Before getting too far Tony looks back and holds up the cards, asking Carla and anyone else silently to play.

"Sure," Carla says. "Come on, Bill. I'll need a partner."

"As long as you explain the rules again," Bill says, following.

Ryan remains at the railing, continuing to watch the town hall they all walked into. Concern paints his face.

"They just need time," you say. "I'm sure they'll want to come with us."

"I hope so. I really do," Ryan says, holding tightly to the railing and staring at the town hall as if willing them to decide to come.

"We'll need to make up their beds and cabins. Want to help me start?" you ask.

Ryan turns away from his watch, hearing the words and nodding in agreement to help.

Hours pass as everyone sits waiting for the villagers to reach a decision and leave the town hall. The sun begins to set in the distance as the first stars appear in the sky.

"There!" Ryan says.

Everyone approaches the railing to look. The island's residents slowly walk out of the town hall and away from the docks, back to their houses.

"They aren't coming." Ryan says, hanging his head.

The hopeful air drains from the crew as they watch the villagers disappear back into their homes, not once looking toward the dock or sending someone to inform you of their decision.

"Ready the ship," you say. "They made their decision."

One by one the crew members pull away from the railing to prepare the ship to sail. Ryan lingers watching the village. He closes his eyes, wishing, hoping, praying.

When he opens them, something is different.

"Wait. What is that?" Ryan asks.

Off in the distance, above one of the homes, smoke rises. A little at first, but then it grows, and flames engulf the home.

"A fire," Tony says. "They must have left a candle lit while they were in the meeting, and it caught the house on fire."

"It grew whenever they opened the door and gave it more air," Chip says in agreement, "We should go help."

The fire overwhelms the home.

"No, look!" Ryan points to other homes where smoke begins to billow out of. "More smoke! And see the people, they aren't running to the fires. They are walking away from them. Coming to us."

The villagers all slowly leave their homes carrying the few things they may need for the trip. They walk down each of their paths, joining one another as they reach the main road leading to the docks.

"They burned it all," Tony says quietly.

Chip nods beside him, both standing reverently as the flames rise.

The villagers reach the docks and walk to the gangplanks and board the ship, joining you at the railing to watch the flames engulf their former home.

"Shall we be on our way?" the leader asks.

"Of course," you reply.

Flames crawl across the island, devouring everything in their path. You watch from the water as the buildings, the fields, the docks, and everything on them burn with an intensity that you can feel on your face from the distance. The smell of smoke lingers across the water as it all burns. Upon finding stored buckets of tar and other flammable liquids, the flames shoot high into the sky and burn brighter than before.

You and the crew watch, mesmerized by the flames, but as everything burns away, all that is left is the scorched earth and tiny remnants of lives lived on the land.

"Where to next, Captain?" the village's leader asks, pulling you from your fire-borne trance.

Are you where you are supposed to be?

From our story we learn of a group of people on their way toward an established goal. Somewhere along the way, after setbacks and disappointment, the group decided that where they were was fine, and they stepped off the path toward their goal. They then sacrificed their vehicle for comfort prior to reaching their final destination. Cortés burned his ships in 1519 after arriving in the "New World." This act removed the option of turning back, which was needed at the time. They were at their destination, turning back could not be an option, and so it was removed by burning the ships.

Have you burned the ships too soon? Have you dismantled them? Are you at your final destination yet?

As in our story, is it time to let go of some of the comforts and crutches you have built and get back on the ship toward your end goal? The people in our story decided to burn everything they had built to get back on course toward their ultimate mission, leaving it all behind for the belief in something better ahead. In Philippians 3:13-14, Paul says, "Brothers and sisters, I do not consider myself yet to have taken hold of it. But one thing I do: Forgetting what is behind and straining toward what is ahead, I press on toward the goal to win the prize for which God has called me heavenward in Christ Jesus."

Have you stepped off the path toward a once spoken goal? If you have, you are in good company, but now is the time to look forward toward the goal like Paul.

Burn the things that keep you from it—the comforts you've chosen instead of the mission. Burn them. Get on the ship. The horizon waits, and the mission is still yours.

Fixed Point Navigation

"Are we lost?" The question hangs in the air—spoken aloud at last by a brave thirteen-year-old girl, though many had been thinking it.

"Not lost. We just don't know where we are... specifically," George, the navigator says.

The map laid out before the group has several points marked throughout the ocean: destinations as well as resupply points and water sources.

"So where are we, generally?" the thirteen-year-old asks George.

"The ocean," a bystander jokes, getting a couple of snickers and several looks of disapproval.

George ignores it, tapping the map, his finger resting on a small port near the southern edge.

"We stopped here last. Sailed north. But sometime last night, we veered off course..." George's voice tightens. "Now we're... somewhere out here."

George circles an expanse of ocean with his finger—empty and vast.

"Why don't we sail north again until we hit land and adjust from there?" another bystander asks.

"We need that next port to resupply water. We have a little cushion, but not enough to go wandering around." George stares into the map, almost through it.

"But we may be exactly where we need to be. Why worry?" yet another asks.

George is frustrated. "We still have several days to sail. If we are a few degrees off course"—George grabs a pencil and starts drawing lines on the map with a straight edge—"over hundreds of miles, those few degrees take us miles off course and we can miss the next island entirely. Sail by it and never even see it." George tosses the pencil down.

"So how do we find where we are specifically when we are in the middle of the ocean?" the thirteen-year-old asks.

"Found it!" The captain charges into the room with something wrapped in cloth in his hand.

"Found what?" George asks.

"We haven't used this in far too long. That's on me," the captain apologizes. "Come to the deck, and I'll show you."

The crew follows the captain up to the deck. George gathers his map and tries to get around them but can't. He is stuck in the mass of people following the captain.

The crowd gathers around the captain as he unwraps the mysterious object in the cloth. It is a weird metal device. He holds it one way, decides that isn't quite right, and readjusts his hands and tries again.

George presses toward the front, trying to see what the captain is doing.

The thirteen-year-old speaks first in the crowd. "What is it, Captain?"

"If I'm honest, I don't know the exact name for it anymore," the captain admits.

"It's a sextant," George pipes up, standing now at the front and able to see. "It helps you find where you are on the ocean."

The captain fiddles with it a little more but can't seem to remember how to use it. He looks toward George and ushers him up to where he is.

"Can you make this thing work?" the captain whispers.

"I think so, but it has been a while—and it works better at night," George admits.

The captain hands the tool over to George.

George fumbles with it, finding his bearings and trying to remember exactly how to hold it and use it.

He begins talking himself through it.

"The sextant was created to help us navigate. You find fixed objects in relation to the horizon and that'll give you a line all around the world"—George finds the sun in the sky and takes a "sight" to find the angle—"but you don't know where on that line you are until you find another fixed object and create another line giving you an intersection. And that is where we should be."

George looks through the sky but can't find another object to sight on. He looks to the crew.

"Check the sky, everyone. We need a bright star or the moon, any object fixed in the sky to sight in on. I know it is daylight, but look hard."

The crew scatters, looking to the sky. Several of them climb up the mast to the crow's nest, looking hard for any star.

"Is that something?" the thirteen-year-old cries out from the side of the ship, pointing up into the sky.

George rushes over to the edge next to the youth. Squinting toward the sky, his breath catches. "Sirius," he says. "Brightest star in the sky."

A soft cheer ripples through the crew as he takes the sighting and records the two angles. Rushing over to the map he laid out, he draws the two angles in relation to the map and puts a dot on the intersection.

"Here we are," George exclaims.

The captain goes straight to work with the new information, shouting orders to the crew, who are more than happy to hop to it.

After the new course is set and things calm down, the captain addresses the crew. "Let us never again forget the tools we've been given. Let us all learn to use them and use them well so that this is never a thing that happens again."

"Hear, hear!" the crew yells.

As Carla finishes her story, several new members of the crew gain a renewed excitement about her lesson on learning to use a sextant.

"I'm going to find the Sirius star," one young student exclaims.

Another student stands to the side, shooting an angle with his sextant, quieter than the rest.

"You getting it okay, Sam?" Carla asks.

"Yes ma'am, but... how could they forget a tool that tells you exactly where you are and helps you find where you need to go? It seems too important to forget."

She smiles at Sam's understanding.

"There are so many reasons why we forget about the tools we've been given. Self-importance, pride, over-confidence in our ability to navigate the seas by feel. If you're out here long enough, you pick up many skills, and they are useful. Leaving our port, most of the crew knows if we aim the ship at the lighthouse and turn north before hitting the rocks and hold a northerly course, we'll be in Dunbar in twelve hours."

"Or how you spy a sea bird with a beak full of fish, you know it is flying to land, and you can follow it there," Sam adds.

"Exactly! All useful observations, but nothing beats the tools we've been given."

The other students have become restless, and it appears the class has ended itself.

"Class dismissed. Leave the sextants here—but they are always available to practice if you like," Carla says.

"Thank you, ma'am," the students say one by one as they lay the instruments down on the table.

You had listened in the background as she taught, learning a few things yourself about navigating by sextant.

"You were the thirteen-year-old girl, weren't you?" you ask, as you approach.

"I really couldn't understand not knowing where you are. If you pay attention to where you were and where you are going you should know where you are." Carla smiles. "But then I grew up and lived more life and found the hundreds of different ways you slowly drift off course. The imperceptible currents and winds, fouling on the ship's hull causing drag, a single broken rope in the rigging, the list goes on and on."

You nod in agreement and say, "Thank you for teaching this class. I didn't want to admit it, but I'm not the most competent with the sextant myself.

"We all have our gifts," she says, smiling. "And we all have work to do building these skills. Just practice, often."

She puts each sextant away carefully in the ornate box they came in.

"You'll always know where you are—even if it's not where you're supposed to be yet," she says, "And that is how you know to move."

A sextant was a tool of the sailing trade—like a hammer to a carpenter or a calculator to a mathematician. Every trade has several tools that are specific to it, but you also have tools that are universal for all jobs. In spiritual terms, these tools are our gifts.

We all have toolboxes we carry with us throughout the day. We fill that box over the years, learning trades and gaining skills that help us move through life. We have a series of instructional manuals for those tools too and for life. We find ourselves aligning to one instructional manual or another. As Christians, we have the Bible, and a helper, the Holy Spirit, to help us and teach us how to use these tools we've been given. First Corinthians 12 outlines spiritual gifts (tools) and their place in our lives. Unfortunately, we can have all the tools in the box at our disposal, but if we never take them out, practice, and hone the skill of using the tool, then how can we expect to be able to do the things God calls us to?

The student at the end of the story asks, "How is it possible that people could forget about a tool so useful?" Unfortunately, this happens every day, day after day. We wander, sometimes out of ignorance, most of the time out of stubbornness because we don't want to do the work to grow the gifts we've been given. It is a choice to engage with the tools we've been given every day and to use them so that we may become more proficient, with the intention of becoming master craftsmen one day.

What is a tool you possess that you don't use often enough? Have you been told you are a great listener, comforter, leader? Whatever you are good at, sharpen that tool and ready it for use because one day, the clouds will part and the opportunity will come—and the world will need what only you were gifted to give. Will your tools be ready?

THE DOLDRUMS

You toss a handful of sand into the air, trying to gauge the wind. The swirling nature isn't helping. Chip and Tony stand by waiting for your decision about the sails.

"Bad memories tied to that... tossing the sand," Mr. Strom says.

Mr. Strom was the leader of the village that burned their houses. While the ship could handle the number of new people aboard it, it was becoming quite snug, giving opportunities to interact like this.

"You lost your wind?" you ask.

"Ay, that and a few other things," he says.

"Would you tell me your story?" you ask.

The ceremony of the captain's actions is intriguing. He wets his finger and holds it up into the air. He stares at it for several seconds as if he was divining some great mystery. After a long minute, he reaches into a barrel of sand near the wheel, grabs a pinch, and tosses it into the air, watching every particle as gravity brings it back to the deck. Several members of the crew stand by and watch, waiting for the orders that would come after this ceremony. After twenty long minutes, the captain speaks.

"There's no wind," the captain says flatly. "We'll try again tomorrow. Mr. Strom, you have the deck."

The captain retreats into his cabin as Mr. Strom steps forward.

"Okay, everyone," Mr. Strom starts. "Today is no different from yesterday. You know what you should be doing."

"Excuse me, Mr. Strom?" a younger crew member pipes up.

"Yes?" Mr. Strom asks.

"The lifeboats I'm supposed to maintain are gone. What am I supposed to do if they aren't there?" the younger crew member asks.

The small crowd looks around at each other knowing what the missing lifeboats mean. Several more crew and their families decided to leave the ship overnight.

Mr. Strom, ignoring the news, says, "I'll find another task for you to complete. Hop to it, everyone."

The crowd disperses, heading off to complete their tasks.

Mr. Strom walks the deck, reviewing the work being completed, sometimes pitching in where help is needed in that moment. His work with the crew did help build morale and boost spirits, but the underlying issue wasn't going anywhere anytime soon. The ship is adrift, and the sails hang like tired flags waiting for wind to fill them.

It had been several weeks at this point, and while Mr. Strom kept a strong façade, he worries how much longer the crew can take the lack of direction and forward movement.

Most of the crew that remains remembers the days the ship carved through the sea, heading from port to port on a very special mission, but those days have long passed. They were holding onto the idea that those days would come again and so they stayed.

But the sails haven't billowed in the wind in quite some time, and Mr. Strom is doing everything he can to keep the ship together. It doesn't help that the captain seems to have no interest in the ship. He comes out and does the little song and dance from time to time, but the joy that graced his face when he would stand at the helm and guide the ship through the sea has gone. There is no interest in the mission anymore, and the ship is dying because of it.

Although, as Mr. Strom walks the deck, anyone passing by would think this ship was alive and engaged. The people are active and work hard completing their tasks, but the ship hasn't moved in days. Several times, Mr. Strom checks the anchor to make sure it isn't an oversight that the anchor was down and that it isn't the culprit for the lack of movement. As Mr. Strom makes his way around that side of the ship, he leans over the edge and checks once more to make sure, but the anchor is right there as it had been.

"What are we going to do, Mr. Strom, sir?" the voice asks from the bow. It is Mr. Smith, one of the oldest crew members. He has been there from the beginning and has spent nearly all of his adult years on the ship.

"I don't know." It feels good to be honest, Mr. Strom thinks, as he gives the first real response since they lost the wind.

"I believe in the mission we set out on all those years ago, but if we aren't on the mission anymore—we haven't served a port in ages—what are we doing?" Mr. Smith, even though frustrated, keeps his tone low to maintain the privacy of the conversation.

"The captain..." Mr. Strom starts.

"Has no interest in this ship anymore, or its mission. We are stuck in the Doldrums." Mr. Smith finishes.

As Mr. Strom leans against the side rail looking out across the ocean, Mr. Smith says matter-of-factly, "He is going through the motions like always... but something's changed. It's in his eyes. The way he looks at things around the ship, the people, the waves, it's different."

Mr. Strom watches the water, how it moves without pattern in the middle of the ocean.

"It is different," Mr. Strom says. "I know it was a slow arrival into this place, but it felt like overnight we were in the doldrums. Santa Luisa wasn't easy for any of us, and I think the captain took it the hardest. He put on a brave face and kept working, despite that failure. I followed his lead, when I should have recommended we port for a time to recover. Part of my job is making sure he takes care of himself when he won't."

"That may be, but his choices are his own, and from what I can tell, he has chosen a new path that doesn't include the mission, this ship, or her crew." Mr. Smith secures a rope as he talks. "Maybe he needs permission to move on. Maybe now is the time you make that recommendation, Mr. Strom."

Mr. Smith moves about his work, leaving Mr. Strom to think about what was said.

Mr. Strom works his way around the deck, stopping at one of his favorite places on the ship. The names had been carved into the wood over time. One day a long time ago, the captain had found a name carved into the railing toward the front of the ship. He had made a big show of it, acting like a swift punishment was coming for the one who had done it. But the captain pivoted and said that marking denoted ownership in the thing, so he carved his name right next to the first and encouraged everyone to do the same. He said taking ownership and responsibility of your ship was one of the most important aspects of being part of a crew, always being willing to hand her off if you're called to, but fighting for her day after day because it is your mission.

So many people's names were carved here now. He runs his fingers over the carvings finding a special one—his name, faded but still there. The decision is clear. He knows what he has to do.

The loud knock on the door startles the captain. Nobody had come to see him absent of the day's ceremonial duties in a long time. He hasn't heard the fifth bell yet letting him know he should see about eating before the cook puts away the food.

"Yes?" the captain barks, quickly covering the charts and papers he's been working on.

Mr. Strom opens the door. "Do you have time to talk?"

The captain looks at the covered paper strewn across his desk. "Of course, of course, come in have a seat." He points to the seat across the desk from him.

Mr. Strom eyes the papers as he sits down, catching a glimpse of the corner of a chart. It was a chart he knew too well. Several questions were answered for him by seeing a small corner of a single chart.

"What is that you're working on?" He lifts the corner of the pages covering it revealing the rest. "Is that Santa Luisa?"

The captain fumbles for a moment trying to come up with a lie, but submits to the truth, uncovering the papers and plans underneath.

"Yes, I've been working on a plan for Santa Luisa." The captain waits for Mr. Strom's response.

Mr. Strom knew there was disinterest and distraction, but didn't realize it was also a new calling that had found the captain. He looks over everything, picking up a few pages with crude drawings on them.

"Are these ships?"

"Yes!" The captain perks up as his drawings are recognized for the thing they were supposed to be. "Actually, they all make up a single ship, but they can separate in several places becoming individual ships when they need to be."

"The shifting tides and treacherous rocks of Santa Luisa." Mr. Strom repeats the infamous line they had heard time and time again associated with the place, before setting sail for the islands the first time.

"We weren't designed to handle a place like that. I believe that's why what happened did." The captain's vibrance and passion shines through. Mr. Strom hadn't seen him like this for years. "We couldn't maneuver like we needed to, and the ship took a beating because of it. Our people took a beating because of it, because of my ignorance."

"It wasn't where this ship was called to be." Mr. Strom lets the truth hang in the air. "It still isn't where this ship is called to be... But it sounds like it is where you are being called to."

The captain slumps back in his large chair thinking about the words. "I know I haven't been myself..."

"As your second, I've felt I've had to carry a vision for you, for this ship that doesn't exist anymore. Talking to the crew and trying to be positive feels wrong, because in my heart I know we aren't good right now. We aren't in the place were supposed to be, and I don't know how to get us there. I don't know how to get it back to where we were." Mr. Strom feels a weight lift off his chest, voicing the feelings that he has carried around for months.

"I do love this ship, I really do"—the captain justifying himself as tears well up—"I've spent years on her, from her construction to her first mission, to now."

"But?" Mr. Strom surmises.

"But I've lost any drive to continue on as the captain of this ship, on this mission. Knowing what I know about Santa Luisa, I can't carry on like nothing ever happened. I've got to try and get back there and help them."

Mr. Strom weighs the honesty. "Then you need to go and do that."

"What ended up happening to the captain?" you ask, as Mr. Strom finishes the story.

"I don't know," he says. "The captain left, and we didn't hear from him again. He was on to another commission, focused, but can't say it doesn't make me sad never hearing from him."

"That's rough," Chip says. "Sailing together for a long time and then never talking to them again."

"It has been rough," Mr. Strom says. "We went from that loss to others, and to... well where you picked us up. I wasn't sure if I would ever feel the wind again."

Mr. Strom grabs a small handful of sand out of the barrel on the deck and tosses it in the air. The wind has shifted and is blowing consistently in a single direction now.

"There's the wind," Tony says. "Let's not waste it."

"Tony, Chip, full sails with the wind, if you please," you say.

"Aye, aye, Captain," they say in unison, turning to tend to the sails.

"Thank you for sharing your story," you say to Mr. Strom, "It's important. And I won't forget it."

Mr. Strom nods, grabbing another small handful of sand and tossing it—not to test the wind, but to feel it on his fingers, see it grab the sand and watch it blow past the ship and back into the sea. He smiles.

Doldrums – Plural Noun; 1. A spell of listlessness or despondency. 2. A part of the ocean near the equator abounding in calms, squalls, and light shifting winds. 3. A state or period of inactivity, stagnation, or slump.

If you've ever set out with a dream in your heart and lost the wind partway there, you're not alone. The doldrums of life are real. This place where every perceivable thing is operating as it should on your ship, but you can't feel the wind anymore. And if you can't feel the wind, I guarantee your people can't either. Sometimes, you even find yourself wishing for a storm—anything to shake the stillness and prove you, your organization, your dream is still alive.

There are several issues you may be experiencing, but the crux of all of them is you are out of alignment with the mission. You have been on this path for a while and in the same way the prevailing winds in one part of the ocean are different than another, so it is for you. Running a small startup out of a garage or preaching to a freshly planted church in a rented out high school cafeteria is different than arriving to work on your company's campus with a small town's worth of employees milling about or preaching five times on Sunday to full services at your church's campus. They feel different because they are very different, and while one may feel like a sweet spot for some, the other can be exhausting and stressful, kicking you out of alignment with the mission.

But don't worry. This is not the first time in history that the leader of an organization had this happen, and I'm sure it won't be the last. A perfect place to start is found in First Thessalonians 5:16-18: "Rejoice always, pray continually, give thanks in all circumstances; for this is God's will for you in Christ Jesus."

These three acts help to ensure you are positioned in a place where you are willing to move to the next step. If you aren't happy, aren't praying regularly, and aren't thanking God for all the blessings in your life, you will likely struggle to hear any truth about your current alignment moving forward. I know that can be difficult. The captain faced that in the story. He was so distraught over past events, he lost sight of what was in front of him, and others suffered for it. It wasn't until someone close to him spoke truth that he realized what he had to do. Winds shift in our life, and when they do, we all have to trim our sails and make adjustments to put ourselves in the best possible position to move forward, to catch the most wind. Or in some cases set off on a new adventure, where the winds are strong again, moving you forward.

A few questions for you to ask: Did the winds shift, and it is time to move on or are you at an inflection point in life? Have things gotten tough and you lack the tools to deal with it so instead of doing the work to learn how to function in this new place you are choosing to give up on your mission? You can't see or feel the wind. Did the wind shift—and it's time to move on? Or is this an inflection point, a moment calling for grit, not retreat? Are you pulling out the oars—or just waiting for rescue?

Throwing a Man Overboard

You awaken to the sound of shouting outside your door.

"You need to let him know!" Tom yells, loud enough and with a tone through the door, trying to wake you up.

"Keep your voice down. We all already decided the punishment in the galley." Martin tries to quiet Tom.

Your room is dark, but you find your way to the door, opening it to see the two of them. Martin stands between the door and Tom, trying to block his way.

"What is the problem?" you ask.

Relief paints Tom's face as he can stand down from this fight. "Martin wants to do something a bit rash."

Martin turns to you, ready to state his case. "The cook's mate has been spreading lies about my daughter. Malicious gossip slanders our family, and I won't have it."

You ponder Martin's statement. "What would you have me do, Martin?"

Martin, hoping you might agree, blurts out, "Throw him off the ship. We don't need that type of behavior here. He never deserved to be here anyway."

"You'd have me cast him into the ocean?" You make sure you are understanding him.

"You don't have to do it, Captain. Several members of our group and I agree and can handle this ourselves."

If Tom hadn't come when he did, the young man would have been swimming already by the sound of things.

"Tom, bring the cook's mate to my quarters please." You look past Martin to Tom.

"Will do," Tom says.

As Tom turns to leave, Ryan and Carla appear from the stairwell, drawn by the shouting.

"Everything all right, Captain?" Ryan asks quietly.

"We're handling it," you nod. "Could you two go to the galley, I think you'll find others there. Keep things calm?"

"Of course," Carla says, glancing at Martin before turning to go.

You stand, staring at Martin, waiting.

Unable to withstand the silence, Martin continues, "Captain, we can't have that here. It is unacceptable, will ruin morale. It will tear your ship apart from the inside out."

"I will speak with him, then with you. Then tomorrow, when we have all slept, I'll address everyone aboard if necessary. Understand?"

Martin, reluctant, finally nods.

"Tell him to come in when he arrives." You turn back into your room shutting the door behind you.

You trim the small lantern on your desk, brightening the room. Shuffling papers aside, you clean up your workspace before you hear a rap on the door, and the cook's mate pokes his head in.

"You wanted to see me, sir?" The cook's mate seems nervous, understanding the havoc on his doorstep.

"Yes. Please, have a seat." You point to a stool sitting near your desk.

He grabs the stool and pulls it closer to the desk, sitting down.

"What are these rumors you have been spreading regarding Martin's daughter?" You come right out with it, trying to salvage what night there is left.

The young man hangs his head and then his shoulders begin to heave, building until he starts to cry. He tries to speak—lips moving, but the sobs fracture his words into unintelligible gasps making it impossible to get a sense of what he is saying.

"Take your time. It's okay. You are okay." You move your chair to the other side of the desk to sit with him, placing your hand on his shoulder, trying to comfort the mess before you.

"I know the things I said weren't honoring, but she hurt me, Captain." The cook's mate breaks down again thinking about the hurt.

"Sarah confronted me about it earlier," the cook's mate admits between sobs. "She told me that lies eat away at everything they touch, like poison."

You nod, unsurprised. Sarah held truth very dearly and fiercely defended against lies.

The next hour is spent listening to his story, very little having to do with the situation at hand, but all playing a critical part in the recent events and how he reacted to unrequited love from Martin's daughter. At the end of it all, you ask him to meet with you twice a day and that he apologizes to any harmed parties, to which he agrees.

You send him out the door. "Tom, can you see him back to his bunk?"

"If it is the same to you, sir, I'm going to start in on the morning meals," the cook's mate says.

"That is fine with me." Turning your attention to a still-angry Martin, you say, "Come in."

You shut the door behind the two of you. The latch hasn't even clicked before Martin starts in again.

"You are letting him go back to work, like nothing happened?"

You gesture to the stool, your voice even. "Have a seat, Martin."

Martin paces a few more times before taking you up on the offer.

"How can he stay when he did what he did? What he said? It is unacceptable."

"I agree, Martin. It is unacceptable." You let Martin hear the words. "He feels truly sorry about his actions and will apologize, specifically to your daughter. Moving forward I'll be meeting with him regularly to discuss the issues that led to his actions. Helping him with some past hurts that he has never dealt with."

Martin hears the words, but you can see it isn't sinking in. "All due respect, Captain, you are wrong to let him stay, and several others agree with me. Letting him stay only shows the rest of your passengers and crew that this type of behavior is acceptable so long as you 'feel bad' afterward."

"Martin, would you have me throw everyone overboard who offends or hurts the feelings of you and your family?" You step it up a notch hoping to reason through.

"Feelings? He slandered her name. We only get one of them, and he worked to ruin hers." Martin is on his feet again, pacing. "I'm done talking, either he is off the ship at the next port or several families are leaving with me."

"Martin, have a seat." You point to the stool once again.

"I don't want to sit," Martin pushes back.

"I didn't ask if you wanted to sit, Martin. Have a seat," you order this time. "I want to hear your story; so many new people aboard I believe I've neglected in making time to hear all of them."

"This isn't about me or my story, this is about..." Martin tries to rage on.

Your own anger builds. "You are right. It isn't about your story, because at the end of the day, all of our stories are the same. Whether you cruised the shallows or dwelled in the depths with the leviathan, we were of the water. By grace we were pulled from the water, made new, all of us. Would you cast a new creation back into the depths, where it no longer belongs? That is what throwing him overboard represents. You, Martin, saying that this person who was made new, not by you, is not worthy of that free gift and would cast them back? Can you not remember the life underwater? Has it been too long, that you no longer remember that we are part of a grand rescue mission? He is sorry beyond your imagination and is beating himself up about it more in this moment than anything you could ever do to him. This is when it matters most. What you would do to him is exactly what is expected under the waves, maybe even worse. But we were made new, to act new, to be new, and I don't know about you, but nowhere in this new world is there room for revenge or malice. There is enough of that below. We are called to be better than that."

Martin is quiet now, somewhere in your monologue, something must have stuck. His head hangs low, and now his shoulders begin to heave. He comes up with tears in his eyes. "I'm still so mad though."

"And that is normal. You and your family were wronged—that doesn't change—but how we face being wronged, how we react is the key. We were born of the water and will always fight against those aspects of our life." You put a hand on his shoulder. "It will be this way for a while, and when those thoughts come up, you have to catch them and call them what they are. Remnants of an old life, not who we are now. Can you do that?"

"I don't know." Martin wipes his eyes. "Where do I go from here?"

"First you need to go back to the others and explain the situation and what everyone should do moving forward. You are an influential member of your group, and the things you say and do matter. Second, go relieve the night helmsman and spend some time thinking about your own story, your journey. I'll see you at breakfast." You give his shoulder a squeeze and stand with him as he exits.

"Thank you, Captain," Martin says.

You lay back down in your bed, thankful for the outcome of the situation. You begin to drift to sleep as someone else raps on your door.

Through the door, you hear, "Knock, knock," Chip calls, unaware of the night's happenings, voice cheery. "Woke up early and grabbed you a cup of coffee, Captain. Made it just how you like it again. Might even be drinkable this time."

You smile. You'll sleep again when you get back to shore.

"For all have sinned and fall short of the glory of God." Romans 3:23

Many Christians know the verse. I'd say that it is in the top ten of verses Christians can quote off the top of their head. Everyone sins; it is an agreed-upon statement to those who believe. If we didn't sin, we would have no need for a Savior in Jesus. We are imperfect; therefore, we have sin.

But what do we do when someone aboard our ship sins against us—when their words strike deep and ripple through our crew? This chapter boils down to how we deal with the sin of a brother or sister. The expectations at times are higher; the hurt is a little deeper. At some point, in each of our existences, we will encounter a time where someone sins against us in the Church, in a ministry, a marriage, somewhere that we feel sin shouldn't enter into. How we deal with that is at the crux of our relationship with God.

The parable of the unmerciful servant (Matthew 18) is the greatest example of this. Jesus says, "Therefore, the kingdom of heaven is like a king who wanted to settle accounts with his servants." Jesus continues to describe a servant who owed a lot of money and begs and pleads to that king for mercy. The king takes pity on the servant and forgives the entire debt owed. Later, the same servant goes out and sees a fellow man who owed the servant a small amount of money. The man begs and pleads the same way the servant did to the king moments before, but instead of forgiving the debt, the servant has the man thrown in prison. That servant gets punished by the king for showing no mercy where he was shown much.

In our story, there is no doubt that Martin's family has been wronged by the cook. I struggled in the writing of this chapter, trying to think of the example I should give. Slander and gossip are a common issue in the Church, but I didn't want it to be cast aside as some minor thing. As we already learned our words can cause great harm. But there is this tendency in the Church to place sin into ranking categories based on how "bad" the sins are.

Going back, this is why I love the parable so much, debt is debt. At the end of the day, the king could have broken it all down into an itemized list of what was what, but it *was* and *is* and *will* continue to be *debt*. We have been forgiven an enormous debt. In the world of the story we're reading, the separation that exists between the water and surface is too great for anyone to pull themselves out. It is only through acceptance of that payment that we can surface and breathe new life into our lungs, grasping that outstretched hand.

But like the servant with the king, what we do with that gift of forgiveness matters. If we aren't careful, when we are harmed, we may reach for the worldly playbook for settling accounts. This is where Martin is at. He wants retribution to fix the wrong against his daughter. As a husband and father myself, I can relate. "Don't nobody make my babies cry." At least that is my gut reaction to harm against my family. In Martin's case, the quickest way to solve the issue is to remove the problem, the cook.

Throwing someone overboard is the easy way out. It is giving up on a person and saying, "It is too hard for me to walk alongside this person, let alone be in the same space as them in the midst of their trials, the time when they need me the most, so I'm sending them out alone into the world."

Some will say, "What about the verses earlier in Matthew 18?" The biblical "guide to making someone walk the plank," or carry out church discipline, up to removal. The crucial part in all of that is repentance. In our story the cook is repentant upon being confronted. As Jesus lays out in Matthew 18, it is as basic as a flow chart gets. Step one, one-on-one confrontation of the sin. If they listen and repent, you have won them over. It lays out the further steps should they not listen, and it ends with the person leaving.

The challenging part of this whole discussion happens not when we as Christians play the sin game I discussed earlier, or when we follow the Matthew 18 flowchart, but when the sin hurts so deeply. The story could have taken a far darker turn—there are wounds beyond words, sins that tear through the soul. For some, those stories are tragically real and painful. It is impossible for me to understand the dynamics of that pain in your soul. An event like that shapes much of your life and how you respond to it. What I do know—and as hard as it is for us to reconcile this truth against the pain we feel—Jesus died for all of us, despite our sin. Despite their sin. Despite his sin. Despite her sin. Jesus, perfect in every way, died for us all.

He did that, suffered that, because of His love for us. A love that once we've experienced it, is hard to put into words, but we try. We try to pass it on to others in how we treat them and the grace that we give. Remembering that the grace we were given is for all, those still beneath the surface and those above. Who are you giving grace to today?

DECOMMISSIONED

The harbor never looked so lovely as when you come sailing into it. Several familiar faces smile at the sight of your ship. They come running to greet you and your crew and to help offload. The smells of the harbor fill the air, a smell of home. You are glad you went and accomplished what you'd been commissioned to do, but also glad to be back.

The process of decommissioning is new to you and takes you by surprise as the last of the passengers disembark. A man approaches you and Tom and hands you papers, decommissioning the ship.

"Good morning! The ship has served its important purpose and will now be decommissioned. It is time to move on to the next thing," the man says without looking up from his clipboard and papers. "Take the day to clear out your personal belongings. First thing tomorrow morning, we'll move the ship out."

He looks through his papers, and upon seeing everything is in order, he starts walking off.

"Wait!" you holler after him.

"It's all in the paperwork. Don't worry. Another commission will come along soon enough," the stranger says as he walks away.

You stand stunned, holding the decommissioning papers in your hand, not realizing the whole crew overheard.

"Can he do that?" Scarlet asks.

"He can," Carla sighs. "You have to remember it is coming from the Harbormaster. He just delivers the paperwork."

"So it's over?" Bill asks.

"Our time on this ship is," Carla says. "But life is far from over."

"Always another commission," Tony starts.

"If you want one," Chip finishes.

"I'm sorry everyone," you say. "I had it in my mind we were just at the beginning of something."

"We are," Carla says. "You don't see it yet, but you will."

"What do we do now?" Sarah asks.

"Gather our things," Ryan says.

"One last meal on the ship?" Chip asks. "We have all that tuna Tony caught."

"I'll gladly give up my"—Tony shoots Chip an eye and a smile—"tuna for the meal tonight."

The day is quiet as the crew goes throughout the ship collecting their things. You notice each member says goodbye to the ship in their own way.

Chip and Tony sit high atop the main mast's yardarm. Occasional laughter makes its way down to the main deck.

Bill catalogs each and every map and chart, annotating what occurred and ensuring the captain's logbook accurately reflects everything.

Ryan lays in his hammock in the hold, swinging back and forth, soaking in the feeling, afraid he wouldn't feel it again for a while.

Scarlet walks every inch of the boat several times. She touches, smells, listens, looks, committing it all to memory, not wanting to forget.

Sarah sits quietly at the front of the ship, sewing something, looking up occasionally and wiping a tear or two away from her eyes.

Carla joins you and Tom at the helm.

"How are we doing, boys?" Carla asks.

You and Tom smile.

"As expected," Tom says, teary-eyed.

"Seems like just yesterday we were calling up to you guys in this ship," you say. "And now it's going away."

Carla smiles and comes in to hug you both.

"I want you to remember something," she says, pulling back. "The ship isn't the mission. It helps accomplish the mission, but the people are the mission. Always have been, always will be. Sometimes the only way the Harbormaster can get us to move on so that He can use us for other things is by taking His ship back. We don't understand it at the time, but we trust it, we trust Him."

Both you and Tom simply nod in agreement, tears answering further.

Carla wipes a tear from her own eye.

"So dusty out here on the water," she says, joking.

"Like a dust storm," Tom says, wiping his own eye.

"How about you boys help me start cooking?" she asks.

"Let's do it," you say.

You and the crew share this one final meal on the ship's deck—simple food, but a time full of meaning. There are laughter and tears, stories shared and lessons learned. It's quieter than usual, and the sadness bleeds into the conversation from time to time. Eventually everyone knows the night is ending.

"What now?" Ryan asks.

"Whatever Harbormaster has next," you say, looking to Carla as she nods in agreement. "Until then, we wait."

"I made us all these. I'm sending one to Harry too," Sarah says, revealing what she had been sewing.

She holds up small patches made from pieces of the ship's sail. She'd embroidered the ship's silhouette onto the fabric and wrote *The Return* under it.

"It's not much," Sarah says.

"It's perfect," every member of the crew says, all getting up to give her a hug.

What do you do when the thing that once gave you purpose, structure, and identity is taken away? When the "ship" you've poured your heart into—be it a job, a ministry, a role, a relationship, or a season of life—is suddenly decommissioned?

There's a strange kind of grief that comes in moments like these. You're not in crisis, exactly. You made it to safe harbor. The mission didn't fail. But something has ended... and it ended without your say.

In the story, *The Return* is decommissioned not because of failure, but because its time was complete. The Harbormaster still had a plan for each of the crew, but He required them to let go of the ship first. The ship was never the point—the mission was. And the mission has always been *people*.

In Scripture, we find a powerful echo of this reality in Acts 13:2, "While they were worshiping the Lord and fasting, the Holy Spirit said, 'Set apart for me Barnabas and Saul for the work to which I have called them.'"

At that moment, Saul (later Paul) and Barnabas left behind the comfort and rhythm of the church in Antioch—a thriving ministry, a beloved community. But the Spirit had another commission in mind. That shift didn't mean the old ministry was invalid or broken. It simply meant they had done their part in it and needed to move on.

We often forget that seasons end on purpose.

The question is not whether God will call us forward again—the question is whether we'll still be clinging to the old ships when He does.

Like Sarah's sailcloth patches, we carry pieces of our old seasons forward—reminders of God's goodness, provision, and transformation. We remember all these things—and then we *wait for the next commission*.

Has something in your life been "decommissioned," and you weren't ready to let it go?

Have you confused your assignment with your identity?

Can you trust God knows what He's doing—even when you can't see the next step?

Waiting for a Knock on the Door

That was almost three months ago, and you sit in your small house wondering why another commission hasn't come. Dust collects on your navigation charts, your boots haven't touched a ship's deck in weeks, and you're beginning to get antsy. You waited patiently at the beginning, but now your frustration has grown with the process. You visited the Harbormaster several times, and each time, He says some version of the same thing: "Something special is coming."

The rest of the crew waited for a time but eventually received their own commissions and moved on. Tony, Chip, Sarah, Scarlet, and Ryan all joined a five-masted clipper called *Cor Dei* sailing for deep waters off the coast of the Shadow Isles. Bill was commissioned as the navigator on the *Caritas*. To Carla's surprise, the Harbormaster requested she set off for Port Angeles to spend time with her family.

Tom, ever the compatriot, stuck by your side. He was waiting with you as he had been told to do from the beginning.

A knock at the door.

This must be it! Jumping up, you rush over to open it.

Behind the door stands the harbor's mailman, Jim, with a small package under his arm.

"I have something for you!" Jim says.

He hands it to you and stands there for a moment, waiting for you to open it in front of him. You roll the package, looking around for a label but can't find anything about where it came from—just your name and the harbor name on it. You pause, and Jim, realizing you don't want to open it in front of him, excuses himself.

"I'm sure you want to open it in private." Jim walks away to deliver his next package.

"Thank you, Jim," you say after him.

He turns and waves as he walks on.

The door clicks as you shut it, all the while staring at the package in your hand. Carrying it over to the table, you set it down, taking a seat in front of it.

You don't want to open it, because you know it isn't the commission you've been waiting for. They don't come through the mail like that, you say to yourself. If it isn't what you're hoping for, the disappointment could ruin your whole day.

You inspect the package again, looking for any clue as to where it could have come from. You even sniff at it and shake it like a kid at Christmas before setting it back down in the middle of the table.

As you reach to open it, Tom bursts through the door. "Heyyo," he greets you while sitting down at the table with mail of his own. Not reading the room, Tom begins going through his own mail. You slide your package to the edge of the table and get up to grab some food.

"I really don't understand some of these letters." Tom thumbs through a few of the pages he received. "I don't even remember meeting these people, but they'll spend eight or nine pages explaining why I am wrong and how everything I said when we visited them was wrong and how they'd like me to be more right next time."

"I'm sure they don't ask you to 'be more right' next time you visit," you say using air quotes.

Tom pulls the exact page out of the stack and holds it up for you.

"You're kidding." You snatch the paper out of his hand.

Sure enough, halfway down the page in bold letters: *IT IS CRITICAL THAT YOU BE MORE RIGHT WITH YOUR STATEMENTS.* You stare at the page for a few seconds in unbelief.

"Who even sent this?" you ask, looking at the backside of the paper for some clue.

Tom looks at the envelope, sits up very proper in his chair. *The Good People of Perfection Key.*

"Ohhh, I remember them." The memories of very prim and proper interactions with the people come flooding back to you. "Weren't they the ones who asked for help resetting their culture?"

"That is they." Tom snags the paper back from you and puts it back in the stack. "That'll be a fun one to reply to."

Tom finishes up with his stack and notices the package across the table. "What did you get today?"

"I'm not sure. I haven't opened it yet." You shuffle dishes around, trying to look busy.

"Well open it!" Tom grabs it and hands it to you.

You look at it for a moment and then tear the brown paper on one edge and see that underneath it is wrapped in a tissue paper to give it some cushion. Your heart sinks, knowing it isn't what you want it to be, but you keep opening regardless. Inside is a piece of paper that reads: *Thank you! We don't need this anymore.*

You hand the paper to Tom. He reads it.

You unwrap and unwrap and unwrap looking, for the center of the thing.

You finally find it.

Tom peeks around the packaging and sees what you are holding. "Is that what I think it is?"

Sitting down, you set the abnormally large oyster shell on the table and the paper note next to it. You both sit in silence staring at the gift on the table.

Taking great care, you pry the oyster shell open revealing the giant pearl inside. The room sits silent as you both stare at the perfect white sphere that shimmers of gold as you move your head and change the way the light hits it.

While only a minute, it feels like an hour before either of you look away from it. Neither daring to touch it. You close the shell and place it back in the protective wrapping.

"Well, that is unexpected," Tom says as he sits back in his chair and smiles. "Something tells me that wasn't what you hoped it would be."

You shoot him a knowing glance. "No, it's better. Like getting a letter from an old friend you thought you'd never hear from again. I've been so..."

"Worried about the next commission," Tom interjects.

"I was going to say busy thinking about the next thing, waiting on it. I hadn't even thought about the pearl divers in I don't know how long." You point at the oyster referencing the senders.

"We all have to move on though, and you're trying to do that. ONWARD! Right?" Tom helps.

"Yeah, but I'm sitting here waiting on the next thing, worrying about it. So much so, I'm forgetting about all that has been done. Or everything I could be doing right now to make sure I am ready for the next thing."

Tom looks at you. "I like learning to build boats..."

You meet Tom's eyes. "No more waiting. Let's help build some boats."

What are we waiting for? This quiet period of in-between is often described as the *act* of waiting. While waiting can be the appropriate activity for a time and patience is a virtue we can all work on, we tend to excuse ourselves from any further *doing* until the thing we are waiting for arrives at our doorstep.

As in our story, we spend days and weeks glancing at the horizon, anxious for the next commission. Praying for an answer, seeking guidance from the Harbormaster, but annoyed at the response. Sitting in a state of waiting because we haven't gotten the exact answer we're seeking.

As Christians, we develop a habit based on the biblical truth of waiting on the Lord. You can find several Bible verses referencing waiting on the Lord. Isaiah 40:31 is tattooed on my arm, and some translations say, "But those who wait on the Lord shall renew their strength..." The Hebrew word *qavah* translates as, "To wait, to hope, to look for, to expect." I can't imagine being able to get anything done if you ascribed to just waiting for an answer before you moved.

But I'm guilty of this: "Well, I can't do this thing until I hear back about that." It isn't an untrue statement, which is how we trick ourselves into being okay with the inaction. But what else could we be doing in the waiting that works toward our ultimate commission? Once rescued, you become a rescuer.

Achieving the goal of becoming a seasoned rescuer takes several steps, several actions, and rarely is there a singular linchpin action holding the floodgates of all other actions behind it. Committing to those actions over time will accomplish that goal. Focus matters. But waiting with no movement isn't focus—it's paralysis.

While you wait, build.

Build your skills. Build others up. Build a boat, whether for yourself or others. Build.

What are *we* waiting for? What are *you* waiting for? Take stock in your past, learn from it and charge ahead toward the next great thing, trusting Him all the way. What is that thing you've been putting off—waiting for the "right" moment to begin? Could it be that the "waiting" season is actually provided to you by God as a season for *preparation*.

THE SHIPYARD

You've never walked through the full breadth of the shipyard before, and now its purposeful design reveals itself. With the last two commissions you had no reason to wander deep into the yard, but this part of the harbor was different.

Large dry docks occupy this portion, areas with all the water drained out where the boats can dock to get at certain parts of the ship's underbelly. Several slipways for launching larger, newly constructed ships are there as well.

As you and Tom are walking, side-by-side berths catch your eyes. You both stop to stare at the construction of two identical vessels—down to the rivets, there's not a single difference between them.

"Beautiful, aren't they?" A man you didn't see before is standing nearby, admiring the ships also.

"They are. But why two exactly the same?" you ask, not recognizing the man at first.

"That's what the commission calls for," the stranger replies, stepping closer with his hand extended. "Where are my manners? I'm Paul, assistant to the Harbormaster."

He shakes your hand and greets you with a big smile.

"Wait. You're the one who handed us the decommission papers for our ship?" you say, recognizing Paul.

"I'm sorry. It is just another part of my job. I've been told I can come off as cold at times, and if that is the way I made you feel, I do apologize. I do this so often it is second nature to me, but I forget it is the first time for some of you." Paul's genuine response disarms your anger.

"She was a good ship, with a lot of life left in her," you say.

"No doubt," Paul says. "But if you were to continue on that ship indefinitely, you may never move forward into a greater ship the Harbormaster has planned for you to build."

"What?" Tom says. "You mean..."

Paul shuffles through papers on his clipboard until he finds the ones he has been looking for.

"Here you are." Paul hands commission papers to you.

"You've had them the whole time?" you ask.

"The Harbormaster gave them to me shortly after the decommissioning of your last ship and said I was to give them to you as soon as you came to the shipyard. And here you are."

You smile, starting to realize exactly how the Harbormaster works.

"He wanted me to take the first step, in faith," you say.

"He's been known to do that," Paul says.

You eagerly unfold the commission—but it takes a moment to make sense of what you're seeing. After you review them, you hand them to Tom and as he looks them over, he has to turn the paper several different ways to try and orient himself.

"It looks big," Tom says.

"Yeah. It's big. It says we are supposed to build in the last berth in the harbor," you say, looking to Paul for guidance

"I'll gladly show you," Paul says.

You follow Paul hundreds of yards down the line. Most of the berths are empty, but a few ships in different stages of construction or repair can be seen.

You stop at one. "What are those holes?" Several holes can be seen along what appears to be the waterline of the ship.

"Cannon fire," Paul says without missing a beat.

"Wait. What? Cannons?" Confusion is obvious in your voice.

"All our ships here are meant for, designed for rescue. That isn't the case with other harbors. Some harbors take pleasure in trying to exploit ships flaws."

"The Harbormaster approved that?"

"Oh no, not at all. The ideas of ship armaments in some harbors were intended to be used to deal blows to the creatures of the deep that attack ships without mercy, but some captains in those harbors have differing views about how best to use their cannons. Such as a disagreement about who should rescue in a certain area." Paul points once again to the ship. "As was the case with this ship."

"They were both trying to save people? And they fired on them?" you ask.

"Typically, they don't waste their time with smaller ships like this. The bigger ships are much better targets, easier to hit, then again, they don't damage easily either."

You stand and stare another moment before Paul begins to move along and you follow. Not much further, you arrive at an aged towering building built around the berth. Paul unlocks the large double doors and pulls them open, entering the workspace.

Inside it becomes apparent why the building is so big. The berth is three times larger than any you walked by.

Paul takes notice at your amazement. "It's the biggest berth we have here in the harbor. You'll notice the system of pulleys and winches all throughout the building that'll help you lift the larger pieces into place. Even with those mechanical assistants, I would recommend you add a few more people to your building crew."

Seeing that you aren't paying close attention, Tom pipes up. "How many would you say is a few?"

"Let me see that commission." Paul walks over as you finish grasping the size and scope of the endeavor. You hand the paper to him.

He looks it over, stopping several times to do some mental calculations. "I'd say no less than eight if you want to be done before the due date for delivery."

"Due date?" you ask, having not seen that anywhere on the papers.

Paul turns the papers toward you and points to a small section in the bottom corner of each page. It reads, *Finished ship to be delivered nine months after project start.*

"From what I've heard about you two, I've no doubt you'll get it done. The number of people helping will expedite the process and decrease that timeline. If you'll excuse me, I need to be getting to the other side of the harbor for a christening."

Paul hands you the keys he used to open the doors to the building. "Good luck. Feel free to come and find me if you need anything."

"Thanks," you say, staring at the keys in your hand.

"Later," Tom says as Paul heads out the door. "Nine months from now there will be a ship sitting there, and we'll be christening it, preparing to set sail on the largest ship in the harbor."

"Where do we even begin?" you say looking at the large empty space before you.

"At the beginning," Tom says.

You shoot a look back at him and then crack into a smile. "Fine then, the beginning."

Both of you stand for a moment. "What's the beginning?" Tom asks.

"I have no idea." You both laugh, relief and awe mingling in your voices. "Crew, I suppose. We are going to need a crew."

"Where can we find one?" Tom asks.

Thinking on it a moment, you both look at each other.

"The Retreat."

You made a move, and lo and behold things start happening. Sometimes stepping out in faith is all we need for the next puzzle piece to show up. In Hebrews 11 we see example after example of faith champions. In verse 8, "By faith Abraham, when called to go to a place he would later receive as his inheritance, obeyed and went, even though he did not know where he was going." Abraham didn't have all the answers—he just had the calling. And that was enough.

As we walked deeper into the shipyard in the story we see a few different ships, including those damaged at sea. Not from the creatures of the deep, but from cannon fire... from other ships. The addition of cannons had been meant to protect and defend against danger, but somewhere along the way an amazing tool is misused and aimed at other ships.

That's the thing about stepping out in faith—while you're moving toward God's calling—you're stepping into a world where other ships may not understand the way you've been called to carry out the mission. It may look different and new to them. It's easy to see this play out in the Church today. Trash talking or bashing other ministries is one of the most common ways this shows up in everyday life. The lines have been blurred so well where we can't tell the difference between a concerned critique and an iron ball of judgement hurtled toward another. Too often, the gunpowder is jealousy—compacted and volatile. Something about the other's success rubs you the wrong way, so you load up a ball and sling it their way.

I am not saying that there have never been issues worth addressing emanating from another church. History has shown us that several large churches would have benefitted from a Nathan or a Jeremiah (biblical prophets) confronting the leaders at pivotal moments in their history, but how the Church handles the confronting is lacking. It is far easier to stand at a distance and lob critiques than to engage up close with humility and precision.

Step forward in faith like Abraham—willing to go without knowing all the details—and keep your cannons aimed at the creatures of the deep, not at other ships on the same rescue mission. As much as stepping out in faith is about movement—it's also about mission integrity, a faith that focuses on rescue, not rivalry. Consider the aim of your cannons today. Do you have critiques of other ministries? What is the purpose of the critique? Is it required for your mission and purpose? Is it meant to tear down or build up? If meant to build up and strengthen, are we taking it to those in leadership who have the ability to make a meaningful change?

FINDING A CREW

The smoky interior of Maggie's Retreat is far more welcoming than its weathered exterior lets on. The thick smell of spices on rotisserie meats and the sound of great conversations make this place special. Several sailors sit near the fire, an older man regales them with a tale of a battle against a creature of the deep.

"The Kraken—because I tell you if it wasn't a Kraken I haven't a name for it—wrapped one large tentacle around the boat, and we struck it and burned it until it released us. Slinking back to the deep, we didn't see it again." The old man holds the attention of the younger. "Until, two days ago. Near here, came a'barreling through the water toward our boat, like it remembered what we'd done."

Several sailors burst out with questions at once as the old man calms them down. The Retreat is busier than usual, you note, as you scan the edge for a booth with Tom. A group is leaving, and Tom slides over to it before anyone else notices it is even available. Tom helps clear away the dishes left and orders two drinks.

"I have a good feeling about this." Tom sips on his drink as he scans the crowd.

Maggie's Retreat was one of several dining establishments in the harbor, but it had the honored distinction of being the halfway house for those just off jobs or ships or both. Its proprietor, Maggie, is the kind woman who greeted you upon arriving in the harbor, and her staff came on a ship from the other side of the world, having left everything due to her home harbor imploding. Truly imploding, if you believe the story as it is told several times a month to any who ask. Comfort is Maggie's gift, and The Retreat was a strong reflection of that.

Maggie aimed to ensure all who entered were welcomed with a smile and all who left did so rested and with a full belly.

"Hello! It has been too long." Maggie always tried to welcome guests herself before assigning a staff member to the table.

"Yes, it has. We're going to be looking for a crew tonight." You understand the power of Maggie's staff spreading the word throughout the place if you can get her on your side.

Maggie feigns upset. "You come here to steal my customers and put them to work?"

"Maggie, if you could help us, I promise you we will stop by every night after work—if nothing else to say thank you again for doing this."

Maggie cracks a smile. "Well, if I get to see you every night while you build a giant ship, what could be better? I'll let The Retreat know you are hiring."

"How'd you know the job is for a big ship?" Tom asks.

"The second the key turned on the lock in the last berth, the news shot through town like lightning. I won the bet with my staff that it was you two. Will you be needing any food while you are flooded with eager applicants?"

You're about to decline, but Tom interrupts, ordering oysters and a parade of finger foods.

Maggie leaves the table and goes to work spreading the news of the job to her staff. You watch as each staff member passes the word to the tables they are assigned. Some of the staff depart The Retreat to spread the word to other establishments across town.

As Tom's oysters arrive, a line begins to form near the table with applicants awaiting the opportunity to discuss a position with you. The Retreat's patrons seem to be multiplying as the room is louder and much more crowded than before.

"I guess I should say something," you say as you look at the crowd.

You stand and the room seems to know the drill, a quiet moves over the crowd. You wait till you see most of the eyes in the room.

"As you may have heard, the berth at the end of the yard is open."

A small cheer cycles through the room.

"We are hiring for the construction of a ship. I can't promise crewmember positions at this time, but your participation in the construction will make you a potential candidate. Experience will be considered, but lack of experience doesn't make you ineligible. I'd rather have ten of the most diligent, hard-working, self-starters who have never built a ship over ten who know what they're doing but never show up to work."

A few friends throughout the room give elbow jabs to their buddies who fit that category.

"That said, the number right now is ten, no more and no less. My foreman here"—you point to Tom, who is mid-oyster slurp but stands, wiping the juice from his mouth—"he'll take your name so you don't have to stand in a line. Grab a drink and some food, and we'll try to get through everybody as quickly as possible."

As Tom scrambles to find some paper and something to write with, you see Maggie give you a slight head nod for the food and drink comment.

You sit back down, grab an oyster and prepare your thoughts about who you need to complete this task.

The next five hours blur into a whirlwind of stories, questions, and unexpected confessions. The applicants span the age gap. One woman brings her newborn with her, ten days old. When you ask what she would do with the baby while working, "He sleeps most of the time," she said. "I'll strap him to me—you won't even notice."

The candidates were quite something and many were qualified to build this ship. The first sorting process was relatively easy. You and Tom discuss those who felt this was a calling versus those who saw it as the next job they could take. Not that those who saw it as a job wouldn't be able to help, but jobs can change all the time. Callings don't tend to shift so easily.

Next you sort by knowledge and experience. Finding those with the calling and the experience would be ideal. They could help assign tasks to those with lesser understanding of the process and could teach and guide as needed.

Lastly, Tom recommends a rather unorthodox, but telling, sorting process.

"Whether we could keep talking to them for hours or are glad to no longer be speaking to them," Tom suggests.

"Seems a bit harsh," you say taking another drink.

"We are going to be working in the last berth on the line from sunup to sundown for a substantial amount of time. I'd prefer to be thrilled to see everyone every day and not dreading another twelve hours with them." Tom lets it sit with you.

"That's fair enough. How about: enjoyed our time with them, but don't need any more time with them."

"You can word it any way you want, so long as we understand each other." Tom waves for another order of oysters.

"Go easy. We have more people to meet," you caution.

The rest of the applicants file through one by one. You strive to give them all equal time, but for some, you know thirty seconds in they aren't the one. You listen intently, asking questions that might reveal some hidden skill—some spark—but leave each conversation still searching. Some want to be a part of something bigger than themselves, part of a world they've never been in, but they haven't done any of the things that would help to qualify them.

As the last applicant leaves the table, you sit forlorn and ponder the thought. Tom excuses himself to deal with some gastrointestinal distress from excessive mollusk consumption.

"What's that face about? I haven't seen this place so excited for a new ship in ages." Maggie sidles into the booth opposite you.

"What makes *me* qualified to tell these people *they* aren't qualified to work on this?" you ask Maggie. She can't help but tidy the plates and cups at the table while she listens.

"Whose name is on that paper, the name of the person who is supposed to build that ship?" Maggie asks.

"My name," you say.

"Then success or failure lies with you. As does the decision. Own that; that is what qualifies you. You decide who gets to help and who needs to move on." Maggie gives you a reassuring tap on the hand as she finishes gathering up the dishes.

"Thanks, Maggie."

Maggie stands, picking up the stack of dishes.

"Don't overthink it. They all know the drill and will understand if they aren't picked."

You nod as she moves off, carrying the dishes with her. You look over the list, close your eyes, and breathe a quiet prayer for guidance. As you move your eyes back up and down the list, the process becomes easier. You remember statements made by applicants that struck you as odd, off-putting even in some cases. Taking that to heart, you cross several names off the list. Thinking again about the skilled applicants, you think back to their attitude, humility, or arrogance, and which way they leaned with their obvious skillset. Several more names are removed from the list.

You look over the list again and pause on one of the youngest applicant's names. Not a single marketable skill presented by her, but the attitude was everything you'd hope for from someone her age. A strong desire to learn, a drive to find a job, and a work ethic that felt like you'd have to make her go home every night and race to beat her to the berth in the morning.

Her name stays, and you continue down the list as Tom returns. He looks over the crossed-out names and nods his head in affirmation as he comes to each one, pausing on a few to think it over before moving to the next. No questions come from him as he works his way to the bottom.

"Anybody else on here not meeting your additional criteria?" you ask.

Tom looks it over. "Nah they're all good. Nobody I can't stomach for the duration. It looks like we got our crew."

"Yes, it does," you say.

You stand up again and motion for silence.

"I want to thank everyone who took the time to talk to us today. Each of you have your own specific set of skills and qualities that you bring to the table. If you weren't picked, I wish you all the best. I know you'll find the right place for you soon. Will the following people please join us over at the table..."

You call the names one by one, and they file toward you. With some of the names you crossed off, it is apparent you made the right choice as they storm off or make a face about it. Others, having a few more years on them, face the news with grace and go about their business of telling stories or visiting with old friends.

Once the group is gathered around the table, you look them over. Not the crew you imagined, but somehow exactly the one you need.

The young girl looks around at everyone and then at you and Tom.

"When can we start?" she asks with a wonder in her eyes.

You look to Tom and then to the rest of them.

"How about right now?" You smile.

Picking the right people. How the heck are we supposed to do it? When we watch movies, we see teams assembling all the time and it feels like the right people needed are exactly where they are supposed to be to accomplish the mission. But how are we supposed to assemble the dream team, the perfect collection of individuals who will not only accomplish the mission, but complement each other's strengths and weaknesses?

When Jesus assembled His "crew," the disciples, He had the benefit of knowing people's hearts, which I'm sure played into the selection quite a bit. But what else did He see in the team? Several of them were hard men: blue-collar types, fishermen, a tax collector, and a zealot into politics or rebellion, but was it their personalities that led to their selection? What can we learn from that?

I think anyone who has dealt with the hiring of individuals can speak to the opportunities you have to see into the heart of a person. In my experience, certain feelings, emotions, moods, and attachments only come from certain types of hearts. A negative heart will leak despondency, while a positive heart will leak optimism. A resentful heart, animosity. A forgiving heart, grace.

In my day job, one of the additional duties I've volunteered for is sitting on interview panels for new applicants. I've conducted hundreds of interviews, each no more than one single hour, and while it is possible to hide the truth of your heart for a time, the more the interviewee speaks, the more the truth of their heart becomes apparent to those listening. Arrogance, anger, humility, tenacity, a small list of the things that become apparent listening to someone speak about the things they have done. It is part of why many Fortune 500 companies conduct several interviews at varying levels, some with additional rigorous testing. You may be able to fake it and hide your true heart for an hour, but try it for ten total hours with two of those over a meal. Breaking bread with people is an excellent way of identifying possible problem areas with a potential candidate. How do they interact with the waitstaff? Are they dismissive of those whom they may consider to be of a lower status than themselves?

Beyond the interviews, even after hiring, many companies have a probationary period that gives the company the ability to let the hired go if it isn't working out.

The problem with most of these companies is they have forgotten what they are looking for in this whole process. The practices are in place, but nobody actually knows what they are looking for. We can all see the glaring issues with candidates that are in the realm of lack of professionalism, inappropriate work behavior, etc. But what about the other 99 percent of candidates who we are processing on a regular basis. What are we looking for?

We want people aligned with our purpose—hearts that beat to the same rhythm, even if their resumes don't. Anyone who seeks a position on your ship who makes statements counter to your purpose may be unfit to sail with you. I know we bounce between analogy and real life throughout this book, but real-world example: If you are trying to build a ministry or non-profit to reach inner-city kids with a safe after-school space, and several of your team members keep steering toward opportunities away from the inner-city, that type of person has no place on your ship. They have missed the core of the mission. It is critical to review the motivations of your staff and volunteers to ensure they are where they need to be. It doesn't have to be a huge confrontation when you identify such a person, it is best for them and for you to get them where they best align in mission and values, whether that is on your ship or somewhere else.

The perfect crew does exist. It may never show up on paper the way we expect. With too many intangibles to consider when hiring, the only way is to sit down and have a talk with them, likely two or three conversations if we're honest. Check with team members to see how they are meshing with everyone.

Ultimately, ensuring you hire those who share in the mission and purpose you've set out on will ensure that everyone on the team is working toward that thing with their whole heart. And that will overcome many issues faced by teams today.

But the Lord said to Samuel, "Do not consider his appearance or his height, for I have rejected him. The Lord does not look at the things people look at. People look at the outward appearance, but the Lord looks at the heart."
First Samuel 16:7

BUILDING A BIG SHIP

"But why does it have to be so wide?" Jerry asks again, still struggling to grasp the science of buoyancy.

Tom restrains his eyes from rolling out of his head and covers the question.

"We need the ship to run shallower—no more than a twenty-five-foot draft—but still displace enough water to carry the weight. Hence, the wide base. It should also provide a good deal of stability in storms as well."

"So the wider it is, the shallower it can go?" Jerry repeats his understanding.

"Yes," you say, grateful the point has landed. "This base needs to be sturdy and solid, having a small draft is key, but we're already going to be running so shallow if she runs aground in places. I want it to be able to take it."

"Iron reinforcement?" Charles asks, speaking up for the first time. As the resident blacksmith, his words carry weight.

"Yes, on all the hull braces, the knees at a minimum and the lowest parts of the hull, but keep in mind it is all a balance. The additional weight and reinforcement come at the cost of draft and navigability," you say while staring at the plans before you.

Tom eyes the group. "Okay. We all have a good idea what we are supposed to be doing for the next few weeks. If you have any questions, please bring them to me. If you need any additional supplies, let me know and I'll gather them all up. Let's get to work." He claps his hands once and ushers everyone toward the door.

With that, the group heads out of the room, confident with at least what the next few days will look like.

"Do you think they believe we know what we're doing?" you ask, still unsure yourself.

Tom thinks on it for a moment, scratching the side of his head.

"I think they trust we are trying our best. And the mission is one I know everyone is behind. So, I think they are good."

Tom grabs his stack of papers, glancing again at the supply list, then the rough timeline.

"I'm going to get started on this, some of these things aren't going to be the easiest to get. See if I can't stay one step ahead of the work so they are never waiting on me," Tom says as he heads off to requisition everything needed.

"You'll figure it out. We all will," you say, settling into your chair and scanning the plans once more. Holding up the main vision for the ship, you think of the good it'll do as you look it over, the people it'll reach.

The next few months are filled with success and failure, hardship and ease, need and abundance. You often find yourself staring at the empty framework stretching into the berth. It's not a ship yet—but the plans remain the guide.

I kept this chapter short because there is an abundance of literature in the world on how to build a thing. From the ever so popular ...*For Dummies* series to books of all shapes and sizes from people who have done the work and built a big thing. The hardest part about building anything isn't the plans. It's keeping the purpose in sight.

Don't build the ship just to build the ship. In our story, the ship was being built and designed for a purpose. Every minutia of the plan was specific to the purpose for which the ship was to perform. Ephesians 2:10 says, "For we are God's handiwork, created in Christ Jesus to do good works, which God prepared in advance for us to do." God created you with a purpose, a plan—not to float aimlessly, but to sail toward something meaningful.

As my wife has built a sizeable real estate company, her business coaches have asked her hundreds of times over the years: "Why are you doing the work?" They want to make sure she is tying the core work to a greater purpose. This helps avoid burnout and reminds the business owner about their big *why* when they are in the thick of the nonsense that can be business ownership.

Whatever your mission is, write the purpose of your work everywhere you go. You will see it every day and never forget why you are doing what you are doing, what you are striving for. When the tough times come—and sadly, it's guaranteed they will—you can remember the purpose and push forward regardless of setbacks, because that mission is too big for you to give up on. The people you'll reach—the lives you'll help reshape and restore—are too important.

THE SINKING OF THE LIFE BRINGER

The Retreat is abnormally quiet tonight as you and your crew walk through the doors. Most everyone in the room is gathered around the fireplace. You hear a voice you faintly recognize telling a story.

Maggie turns, hearing you enter and breaks off from the tale, coming to greet you.

"Such warm cheerful faces can only make this dark day brighter. Please take whichever table you like, and I'll bring your drinks." The room is dim, but Maggie's eyes shimmer with unshed tears.

The rest of the group goes to take a table, but you break off to talk to Maggie as she returns to the bar.

"Maggie, what's going on? Who's talking?"

She fills a drink for the table, pausing trying to say something, but not finding the words. She gathers her composure.

"It's sinking." The two words are enough to throw her deep into her feelings.

Your mind reels: *It must be a ship she once sailed on—maybe the one that brought her here, or another from the harbor.*

"What ship, Maggie? The one that brought you here?"

She shakes her head, no.

"The *Life Bringer*." Her tears pour out now as she comes around the bar to hug you, burying her head in your shoulder, crying.

You hug Maggie, trying to console her, but all the while thinking you must have heard her wrong.

The *Life Bringer*, the giant ship you encountered after being pulled from the water yourself. There is no way it could be sinking.

You recall Maggie talking about the *Life Bringer* before; it came alongside their ship at one point and helped. That is what the *Life Bringer* did: it helped any and all that asked for it. It not only drew thousands to the surface, but also poured itself out—tenfold—to help build countless other ships to do the same work.

Maggie pulls back and finishes the task at hand.

"Here I am supposed to bring comfort to my patrons, and you have to comfort me," she jokes, filling the glasses.

"You do it for everyone. Let us do it for you from time to time," you say as you watch the small group around the fireplace begin to disperse. Seeing the face of the man behind the voice for the first time, you recognize Collin, the man in the lifeboat you helped pull in so many people.

You approach him, unsure if he'd recognize you. His stare into the fire is one you've seen before. It's not how people tend to look into a fire, but instead, he is staring into the soul of the fire, back to the wood as a sapling, maybe even a seed and the tree before it that the seed was birthed from. Staring as if lost beyond thought—like something gripping his mind and refusing to let go.

"Collin, right?"

He looks up at you, a hint of recognition in his eyes.

"This is the second time you've shown up when I need help. You followin' me?" He cracks a small smile and stares back into the fire.

"No, this is my port, where I landed after we met." Silence hangs between, both unsure what to say. You decide to break it. "Can I get you some food, another drink? I know you just spoke, but if it isn't too much, I'd like to hear what happened. When you're ready."

He takes you up on the offer of food and drink. You let Tom know you're sitting with Collin tonight and for him to take care of the crew.

You sit in silence for a long time with Collin, eating. He asks a few questions about your time since he last saw you. You share about the shallows, the circuit around the sea on *The Return*, and the ship in construction right now. He nods and listens to your stories.

As you sit in silence, you can tell he tries to speak a couple times but stops himself. The third time it happens, you speak.

"Some stories are hard to start."

Collin thinks for a moment. "I don't know where to start. There is what you know, and when you knew it, but so much more has come to light since the actual explosions on the ship. The story started years before."

"Explosions? I had assumed it was attacked or maybe hit something?"

"It'd been attacked in the past, but this was different. The first explosion blew a small hole in the side of the ship, which started a chain reaction of explosions blowing through several decks on the port side, half below the water line. We all thought we'd been hit at first, but looking at the damage, it had all blown outward. It came from within. Regardless, in the moment there was confusion and fear. Damage control began immediately." Collin stares into his drink swirling the remnants, then downing it.

He continues, "You never think about having two different damage-control plans. I mean an explosion from the inside; how could that even happen? Who would let that happen?"

"What exploded?" you ask.

Collin chuckles to himself then signals the waitress to ask for another drink. "Two decades worth of toxic combustible barrels."

"What? Two decades? What about inspections?" You are amazed and astounded.

"You can inspect the ship, but if you don't ask the right questions and look in the right places it is pointless. And... when the captain is the one storing the barrels..."

No words from you. You sit back speechless at that revelation. Silence hangs over both of you. Now you are the one trying to find where to speak and unable to find the words. Collin notices.

"That's it exactly, where I'm at in my head. More questions than answers. After the explosions, but before we knew everything, I stood up there, in front of the whole crew with the captain, in 'solidarity' to fix things. He denied the rumblings that the barrels were his, that he had anything to do with it. That the explosions were a planned attack by old crew members who had left the ship angry about this or that."

The waitress brings Collin's drink, letting both of you pause a moment.

"When did you decide to abandon ship?" you ask.

"After the initial explosions, there was one more big one. Months later, that tore through any repairs that had been done. The other leaders and I had searched the ship and conducted our own investigation but missed it. I couldn't continue on in a place I had failed to save."

"Failed? It isn't your fault. The captain knew the dangers of those barrels and continued to store them in places he knew would cause damage if they ever blew." You defend Collin, seeing he is in a bad place.

"For my part, I failed the crew. I'll carry that weight—up here"—he taps his temple— "probably for the rest of my life. Wondering if leaving was the right thing to do. Running away never seems like the right answer."

"It wasn't running away. Sometimes we are too close to something to do what has to be done. The only way it will be done is if we step away from it and let someone else." You think back to similar decisions you've had to make. "Where is the ship now?"

Collin looks up at you surprised. "Out at sea. Last I saw of the *Life Bringer*, it was listing to the port side. I heard all the leadership stepped down and outside help had been called to conduct another investigation. Meanwhile, new leadership is being selected, and they have an acting captain."

"So, there is hope for it?" you ask.

"Hope? Maybe. But the ship will always bear the scars—visible to all those who see it from above and below. I don't know what's next for the *Life Bringer*, but I do know it'll be a long tough road, and it may never get back to full efficiency."

"If it only saves one," you say, raising your glass.

Collin's nod is slow, but resolute. "Then it's worth it."

You discuss several other lighter things throughout the evening, and as the night closes and The Retreat starts shutting down, you can see it is time to go.

"I don't know what your plans are next, but you are more than welcome in our berth. Help with our build if you want."

Collin takes in the offer. "I appreciate it, but I think I'm going to solo sail for a while. I have a couple commissions I've been sitting on far too long, and this gives me the time to complete them."

"The offer stands regardless. Even to come see our progress and maybe give any advice, we'd love to have it."

You stand to go. "Thank you again for taking the time to tell the story."

"I have a feeling I'll be telling it for a while." Collin pauses, extending his hand to shake. "If it only saves one."

You shake his hand. "Then it's worth it."

Luke 12:2-3 tells us, "There is nothing concealed that will not be disclosed, or hidden that will not be made known. What you have said in the dark will be heard in the daylight, and what you have whispered in the ear in the inner rooms will be proclaimed from the roofs."

There are two tragic but funny truths that I've seen throughout the years related to Church scandals. The first: people always seem shocked by what happened. Years ago, it made sense, but today in this digital age it feels like all things are found out eventually. In the Church, the same shocked people can quote, "For all have sinned and fall short of the glory of God." But can't believe it happened in their church. The second: if you spend any time reading the Bible, you'll find that all of the Biblical heavy hitters failed at one time or another. David with Bathsheba and again having Bathsheba's husband killed; Abraham doubting God and having a child with Hagar; Paul was called Saul and killed many early Christians; Moses's temper got him in trouble when he killed the Egyptian and again when he struck the rock later on; Noah got drunk; Sampson liked prostitutes; Peter denied Christ; Thomas lacked faith. The list goes on. Perfect examples of how imperfect we all are.

Knowing what we know from the Bible we shouldn't be too surprised about people's shortcomings. Disappointment is a part of it, but no great shock over what transpires. The real question I have is why the barrels from our story can be more explosive than others. In the Christian walk, it is understood that sin is sin; in the secular world, there are basic agreed upon moral standards that most adhere to. Yet some sin or moral wrongdoing is packaged in these explosive barrels almost like a ticking time bomb waiting to explode. It is more about how it is all packaged than the thing itself.

On April 15, 2013, two bombs detonated near the finish line of the Boston Marathon. From the bomb remnants the FBI pieced together that the explosive material inside the bombs was the pyrotechnic powder from inside fireworks, and it was all packaged inside of a pressure cooker. Three people were killed and hundreds injured by how these bombs were packaged. Nothing placed inside the pressure cooker or the cooker itself was created with the intention of death and destruction, but it was packaged in such a way as to cause maximum damage.

The same applies to our wrongdoings. The quantity and way we "package" or hide and conceal have a direct effect on how much harm it causes. Either way, it causes harm, but when we bury it in large quantities in a confined space, and a match ignites it, it blows up, changing the landscape forever. The final element is the proximity of others to the detonation. Those closest to the blast are the most affected. If you've seen any explosion episode of the show *MythBusters*, then you remember them using the little pressure rupture discs to see if a person could survive the pressure wave from the explosion. Not unlike our world, the explosions our sins create will cause pressure as well and not all relationships will survive the explosive pressure when our sins are alight.

So how do we fix this? How do we minimize damage? The easiest answer is to not sin, but given one of our primary understandings from earlier is that all have sinned and will continue to sin (though, we hope less). We need to know what to do with our sin when it happens. Continuing with the explosive material analogy, we need an explosives disposal team. My time in Iraq was spent in a Tactical Operations Center in Tikrit, where about once a day there was a large explosion or "controlled blast" that shook the whole center. All the ordinance, or old bombs and explosives, that had been recovered over the last week were placed out in the middle of nowhere, a safe distance from any living thing and detonated.

Sin must first be acknowledged—named plainly—and brought into the open where it can be dismantled. We aren't always the best at labeling our own sin as sin, so this is where having someone who loves you, wants you to be the best you, and knows God has a plan for you needs to step in and speak truth into your life. Luke 17:3 tells us, "[I}f your brother or sister sins, rebuke them; and if they repent, forgive them.

It sounds easy enough and I can write it like it is nothing, but let me tell you this is where everyone struggles. Someone reading this right now is saying, "I bring my sin to God and ask for forgiveness and I repent and that is that." Or, "All my sin was forgiven when Jesus died on the cross."

Neither is wrong. But doing nothing to prevent repeat sin? That's spiritual negligence. James 5:16 says, "Therefore confess your sins to each other and pray for each other so that you may be healed. The prayer of a righteous person is powerful and effective." The verse before in James is talking about the power of prayer, and if someone is praying for your sin in faith, it'll be forgiven. This is why we confess, so we have the power of others' faithful prayers over us. James 5:19-20 says it best: "My brothers and sisters, if one of you should wander from the truth and someone should bring that person back, remember this: Whoever turns a sinner from the error of their way will save them from death and cover over a multitude of sins."

Owning our mistakes with ourselves is difficult, which I know means to share with someone else is that much more so. Even harder is asking someone to hold you accountable and a near impossible feat is then being 100 percent honest with them regarding every element of your life moving forward. It goes against our very being of independence. It isn't the small things either. It is the big dangerous barrels we don't ever want to talk about. It comes down to a thing we've faced since childhood. We don't want to be judged or looked down upon. Consider that no parent ever has to teach their child to lie; children know how to do it inherently out of self-preservation. And so, we hide things, we grab a mask and put on makeup. We splash some perfume and try to cover up the stench from things we've done or the places we've been, the explosives we've hidden away. For the sake of the ship—and the souls aboard—stop storing what should have been surrendered long ago. Take it someplace safe, with safe people. Dispose of it all and then establish a plan to be accountable to never storing such things again.

THE GRAVE COST OF FOULING

The ship's young apprentice takes another deep breath and vanishes below the surface. Feeling the hull with one hand, he follows the curve of the ship till he comes upon the thing he was there to remove. Barnacles. In his other hand he carries a tool to scrape. He hammers the hard shells with the butt of it then scrapes the bodies of these hitchhikers off with the other end. It's time for more air.

Maybe two inches had been cleaned off in that go-round, and he goes back again and again until the job is done.

"Ten tons of weight those little buggers can add to the big ships if you don't do anything about it." The old shipwright sneaks up behind you as you sit eating your small lunch of steamed mussels and bread.

"Slows you down quite a bit, I imagine." You offer a mussel as he sits down next to you.

"That, and can alter your course, added pressure and stress on your steering as you are fighting against the current hitting them. It's called *fouling*." He enjoys a mussel while watching the young man dive again and again working to clean the ship.

"What's the best way to keep them off in the first place?" you ask.

The old shipwright thinks on it for a moment, then smiles.

"Never put your boat in the water." He laughs.

You smile and shake your head, nudging him with your elbow.

"Regular cleaning can do it, before they become a more serious problem," he says.

"Every month?" you ask.

He smiles again. "You young folk want the equation for everything. It's not that simple. Just keep an eye on it, checking it from time to time."

"I don't want it to mess anything up," you say, thinking about more than just barnacles.

"I know I was joking when I said it, but it's true: if you put a boat in the water there are going to be many things you have to deal with. Fouling is just one of them," he says.

You both watch the boy dive again and again, cleaning the boat.

"There are paints that can help keep them off, but nothing works forever, and if you count too much on one thing to fix it, you'll end up with the same problem again." The old shipwright takes another mussel for the road and stands up.

"Thank you. I miss these talks," you say as the old shipwright walks back toward his in-progress ships.

Fouling paint. You make a mental note as you watch the ship's apprentice go below the surface again, cleaning the accumulation of what looks like ten years' worth of sea life growth.

Billions of dollars every year are spent on the removal of sea life from vessels in the shipping industry. The cost of fuel to overcome the drag added by these fouling hitchhikers is astronomical over time. In the same way, organizational "fouling," or added programs, can weigh on the overall mission and vision of a church or organization. Now don't hear me wrong, not all of these programs are crusty ocean dwelling hitchhikers. Many have a great purpose behind them. But if they don't align and help drive the mission and vision of the organization, they will weigh on that mission and vision and at a minimum water it down, and worse yet take it far off course.

The early Church struggled with its own fouling—when different groups began adding rules that clouded the simplicity of grace. Paul addressed this several times throughout the New Testament discussing the division and distraction such things caused. It was a form of fouling that removed focus on the main thing which was Jesus Christ.

And the worst fouling? Comes from individuals at the very top. Those in leadership will typically go unchallenged when adding organization fouling of their own design. This is why it is critical that leaders have people in place with permission to challenge them.

Beyond that, every person in an organization should be able to, on the spot, recite the mission and vision of that organization, especially those in leadership positions. Once everyone knows it, decisions become simpler: will this move the ship forward—or drag it off course? This simple implementation will allow you to spend less time scraping barnacles and more time chasing after your big mission.

Therefore, since we are surrounded by such a great cloud of witnesses, let us throw off everything that hinders and the sin that so easily entangles. And let us run with perseverance the race marked out for us, fixing our eyes on Jesus, the pioneer and perfecter of faith.
Hebrews 12:1-2

HAULING OUT

The harbor is quiet this morning. Typically, several ships a week resupplied here, taking shelter from the harsh seas and fall storms. They hauled out for repairs, restocked, and waited for a break in the weather before heading back out.

You and Tom stroll through the streets, making your way back to the ship when you see a curious sight. A young man, early twenties running full sprint, arms full of supplies as if he is trying to catch a ship, but none are moving. In fact, there is one lonely sloop moored at the end of the dock, but he is running as if to catch it.

"Can we help?" you call as he approaches.

"Bring this please," he says as he drops all the supplies at your feet while he runs faster now toward the ship.

You and Tom look down at the supplies, then at the young man now running away, and then at each other and laugh in disbelief at what is happening.

"Never a dull moment," Tom quips as he bends down to pick up the supplies dropped at your feet. You do the same, dividing the supplies between the two of you, which ends up being more than one would think a person could carry at that pace.

The young man had dived onto the ship, fumbling around in the small cabin, the sound of water splashing could be heard.

As you and Tom get closer, you can see the young man swapping between bailing water like a mad man and pumping water out from below his ship. You can now see how low the ship was sitting and how any more seawater would have capsized the whole thing.

Tom hurries along, setting the supplies down on the dock before jumping down onto the ship to help.

"I'll pump; you bail," Tom says to the young man.

You set your armful of supplies down next to those that Tom had placed and survey the ship. The ship's outside gleams with care. Well-kept and clean, with what looks to be fresh paint above the surface.

"Any room for me in there?" you call down to Tom.

"Nah. Check the port bow," Tom hollers.

"No that really isn't necessary. She just takes on a bit of water now and then," the young man retorts.

Tom balks at the notion.

Without further discussion, you strip down to your skivvies and drop yourself into the water toward the front of the ship, making your way around the bow to the port side feeling for possible issues as you go.

The damage is felt from the outside, without seeing it firsthand it is hard to tell the full extent, but all along the front of the ship, there are critical issues. In places, the cracks and holes are large enough to feel the negative pressure of the water being sucked into the ship like water through a reed.

By the time you pull yourself out, the ship is much higher in the water and much closer to safe, for the time being, than before.

"What do you say we get you a berth and haul this thing out for some repairs?" you ask now that both Tom and the young man can take a breath.

"Oh, I don't think so. I'll manage," the young man replies, scooping out another bucket of water that filled up the bottom in the time it took for you to suggest the repairs.

Tom can see you getting frustrated and steps in to ask the most important question: "How long have you managed like this?"

"What month is it?" the young man asks.

"October," Tom replies

"Three years next month."

His statement hits you and Tom like a ton of bricks.

"You've been dealing with this for three years? When do you sleep?" you ask.

"When I can. Sometimes I'll use more ropes to tie up so when the tide goes out, I'll catch a break. Or if I'm really hurting, I'll run aground if it's safe." The young man's face looks worn down for someone his age, and both you and Tom can see it.

"If it's money, we'll see about the berth. It won't cost you anything for that, but the work to fix it will take time and effort on your part," Tom suggests.

"I appreciate it, but I can't do that. It's mine to deal with, and I'm dealing with it," the young man says. There's a long pause, the only thing heard is the water dripping into his ship. He empties another bucket of water out of the bottom of the ship.

Tom has that look on his face where he wants to say several things but catches himself.

"Well, my name is Tom, and this is my captain. If you change your mind, know that is a standing offer, and you can take us up on it at any time, whenever you're ready."

"Thank you both. I should be getting underway while I have the wind." The young man shakes both your hands and goes to load the supplies from the dock.

You and Tom help him and watch as he leaves the port tossing a bucket of water over the side every so often until he is out of sight.

There are no words as you put your dry clothes back on and walk with Tom to your berth, another quiet day in port.

Hauling out, or removing your boat from the water, is a task that most ships could use on an annual basis. It is a time to clean, repair, repaint, tend to a part of the ship that hasn't been seen by anyone since it went in the water. It's messy, inconvenient, and often exposes more than you expected. But without it, cracks widen, and storms can win.

In our story, the cost of hauling out for the young man is too great. Hauling out would give him a much-needed break and could save lives and further heartache down the road, but he doesn't want to take the time to deal with the underlying issue, so he copes. We all have areas in our lives where we could stand to haul out and conduct a thorough accounting and review of repairs needed.

A great place to start is to identify an area in your life that hasn't been clicking. If you aren't sure what those areas could be, start with the seven circles from *The One Thing* by Gary Keller and Jay Papasan. In it they list the seven circles as your spiritual life, physical and mental health, personal life, key relationships, job/work, business, and finances. Pro tip: The area you don't want to deal with is likely the area that needs it the most.

Once identified, the tendency will be to attempt to fix it yourself, but that isn't hauling out. That is maintenance, and it is important, but it isn't going to get to the root of the issue. We all can and should perform maintenance tasks on a regular basis to help lengthen the time between haul-outs, but regardless, a haul-out will be needed in every area of your life at one time or another.

Proverbs 27:17 says, "As iron sharpens iron, so one person sharpens another." A haul-out requires an expert, someone who specializes in hauling out. For your spiritual life, it may be a pastor who can help you name the sin you've been too afraid to say out loud; for your marriage or other close relationships, a seasoned counselor who can trace the cracks that formed when you weren't looking, someone who has helped others deal with issues much like your own; for business, perhaps a coach or mentor who can help you see the areas that need repair and then the path forward to achieve the goal of restoration.

The second thing a haul-out requires is some amount of time dedicated to the act of hauling out and everything that entails. How many marriages have fallen apart because somewhere in the "busy"—work, life, kids, hobbies, habits, addictions—it stopped working. I'd argue that most marriages don't stop working, but people stop working on their marriages. I'm not naïve. I understand that doesn't mean heartbreaks won't come, that betrayals, arguments, and a myriad of other challenges go away. But if the work is being done—dedicated, committed and focused work—the more likely the ship that is your marriage will weather the storms because you'll sail into the storm in a vessel that's sound—tested, sealed, and ready to tackle the waves.

So what are you waiting for? It's time to haul out. Not someday—today. Before the storms hit. Before the cracks in your hull lead to catastrophe. The sea won't wait, and neither should you.

THE MISSION TO THE FEEDING GROUNDS

One cold morning out of the blue, you receive a knock on your door. You open it to find Tom and an older woman you recognize as a captain but can't recall her ship's name. They stand for a moment, unsure who should speak first. Having seen this a time or two now, you know what this is.

"Where do you need us to go?" you say softly, relieving her of the burden of asking.

Tom puts his arm on her shoulder, encouraging her to respond.

"*The feeding grounds*," she replies—the name alone sends a chill through you. You've heard of the dark waters that make up the feeding grounds.

"I know it's a lot to ask, but my crew isn't ready for that," she says.

She holds out the papers, hands shaking still from receiving them in the first place. You take them, squeezing her hand as she releases them to you.

They are standard papers, except for one portion you hadn't seen before.

Rescue & Recovery is written on the papers. You'd only ever seen the rescue portion. Reading through the recovery rider, you now realize why this captain is shook up and why her crew may not be capable of carrying out this task.

"Is there anyone on your crew that would be willing to join us for this?" you ask. "Anybody ready?"

She thinks for a moment and nods in reply. "I think two of them would. I didn't even want to bring it to them, because they would all say yes, whether out of guilt or purpose, but it wouldn't be wise."

You glance at the papers again before addressing Tom. "You think the team at the berth can handle the build without us for a few days?"

"They'll be fine. Probably appreciate it, honestly," Tom jokes.

You look into the captain's eyes before speaking the words you've learned from the other captains.

"I'll honor this commission like it was my own. Harbormaster as my witness, I will do everything I can to see it done," you say to her. "Tom will check in with you about the helpers."

She thanks you and Tom before setting off down the street. Tom watches her as she goes before turning back to you.

"Sorry to bring it to you like that," Tom says, scratching his head. "But I had to help her."

You wave it off. "Don't apologize. I'd do the same thing. The Feeding Grounds, huh?"

"Are *we* ready for that?" Tom asks.

"We'll see my friend; we'll see," you respond.

It doesn't take long to find a crew, hard men and women that come from the same waters you are traveling to. Many of them eager to help see others pulled from the depths. Without much fanfare, you and the small crew set sail for the dangerous waters, the Feeding Grounds.

"It's coming back around!" Tom warns.

You all watch as the large fin glides through the water on its way back to the man treading on the surface in the middle of the Feeding Grounds.

"Swim!" you yell.

The man looks at all of you, then at the beast in the water, looking back he yells.

"I got this. Don't worry about it. Not a problem." The man readies himself as the beast gets close.

You start beating the water with the oar and yelling at the top of your lungs. "Get away from him!"

The rest of your party follow your lead and make all sorts of loud noises, trying to scare the beast away. They grab whatever they can to hit the water and try and knock the beast out of its locked concentration on the man.

"It's not working," you say, looking for any other option.

You move to jump in, and Tom grabs you. You struggle, but know he isn't letting you go.

The beast is almost on top of him. His eyes fill with worry as the enormity of the creature draws close. Without a word, the man is pulled beneath the waves and the beast with him.

You sit, staring in silence at the spot where the man was moments ago. The surface is calm like nothing was ever there.

A couple of the man's friends in the boat start to cry; silent tears turn to sobs. You continue to stare at the surface, tapping Tom's hand to let you go as you sit up, not blinking, watching the spot where the man was. A tear reaches your cheek, and you wipe it off.

"Why didn't he listen to us? What a fool," you say, your resolve hardening as the words cross your lips.

No one disagrees, but the look of "too soon" can be seen from several on the boat.

"We can wait a while, no? See if he finds a way back up. Whatever it takes." Tom's words are true, but you cringe at the use of them against you.

The battle inside you rages as you know the proper and good response, but it takes what seems likes hours to get it right in your head.

"Whatever it takes." You say the words, but in the moment, you aren't committed to them.

You sit down at the end of the boat to rest, closing your eyes so you don't have to see the people you helped save. You wrestle in your mind with the "why," replaying the scene in your head to see if you could have done anything else or if the man was a fool who wasn't ready to make the choice. You feel convicted about your thoughts. You realize that you've never experienced a battle with a predator of the deep. You've encountered them related to other people but never had to stare into its dark eyes yourself, knowing that it was there for you and only you before making the choice to let it take you to the depths and hold you there, gnawing at you until nothing remains.

You wake with a start, wondering when you fell asleep.

The sun has set, and the boat floats on the dark water.

As your eyes adjust, you can see by twilight most of the boat is asleep. Tom stands watching, like a statue not looking away from the water. His lips moving as if talking, but no words coming out.

You stand and move toward him, he notices, but doesn't look away from the water. He acts like he wants to say something but doesn't.

"I'm sorry." You break the silence.

Tom still has no words as he watches the water.

You stand with him, watching the spot on the water where the man last was.

"We're going to have to head back in the morning, aren't we?" Tom speaks.

"We have to help the others back, yes. We could wait till mid-morning, maybe even noon, but at some point, we'll have to call it," you say.

"We can't help save them all. I know this, but will it ever not hurt this much when we lose one?" Tom struggles to get the words out, shifting on his feet as he stares into the water.

"I hope not," you say, squaring your shoulders. "We'll struggle, get mad, fight the feeling to give up. But I've seen the tears the Harbormaster sheds over each and every one lost at sea. He knows them all, whether they know Him or not, and He sends ship after ship to them to try and bring them home."

"I don't know if I'm strong enough for this." Tom's honesty comes through.

"None of us are," you say. "But I know this is where I'm supposed to be, and the strength will come when I need it."

"I'm sorry I held you back from jumping in." Tom makes eye contact with you.

You put an arm around his shoulder.

"We all do what we feel is best in the moment with the information we have. And I trust you did just that. I don't question it." You give him relief with your answer. "Besides I could have pulled away if I really needed to."

You jab him in the ribs.

"Oh, of course." Tom jabs back.

The two of you stand watching the water.

"Why don't you rest. I'll stay up," you say.

Tom nods and moves over to where you had been sitting, closing his eyes, trying to calm his mind. His lips return to the silent movement, praying, until sleep catches up to him.

You watch the water and the stars as they reflect across the ocean. Tiny points of light reflecting, bouncing from wave to wave. After watching for several minutes, the water's movement plays tricks on your eyes, making you think there is something there, but nothing has surfaced.

"He isn't coming up." The familiar voice shocks you out of your gaze.

Charlie had surfaced right next to the boat.

"Charlie?" You whisper as to not wake anyone.

"Yep." He pulls himself up and you help him into the boat. He stands next to you dripping.

"Did you see anyone down there?" you ask, the initial surprise of seeing Charlie fading fast.

Charlie wants to speak but only nods his head and repeats himself. "He isn't coming up."

"But he could. If he chose to, he could," you defend.

"The same way the Harbormaster could drain the seas today if He chose to, He could, but He doesn't." Charlie is angry.

You sit with that for a moment, not sure what to say, and watch the water with him for a long time.

"The last time we met, you struck me as someone who knows the answers to questions like that, but you don't like them. The answers, that is." You don't want to fight but rather to let him sort through it.

"What, that we created the sea, the separation. But He provided us the ability to open the spigot and fill the ocean. Why, if He wanted us with Him, why would He do that?" Charlie argues, more with himself than with you.

You sit, knowing he is chewing on his own words and the knowledge.

"I know He gave us a choice, but if He cares so much, why would He let that man choose to live here." Charlie points to the depths. "Where sharp teeth and death linger, waiting for the next person to arrive. These Feeding Grounds."

"Why are you here?" you ask.

Charlie sits with the question for a long moment.

"I'm looking for something." Charlie's eyes watch the water.

"What are you looking for?" You turn to him.

"I'll know when I find it," Charlie says as he moves back to the edge of the boat. "If I see your guy again, I'll let him know you're still here and to come up, but prepare those aboard for a recovery, not a rescue. Probably the only way he is coming up."

"Thank you for trying, Charlie. It was good to see you—even under these circumstances. Be safe," you say.

Charlie doesn't look back, but nods as to say, *You too*, and dives into the water, disappearing into the depths.

You stand watching the water again as before. Praying for Charlie, the man, and all those who choose to live here, that they would see the lights and come up.

Later that morning, as the golden sun lit across the surface of the glassy water, the man did come to the surface. He surfaced the way Charlie said he would. The recovery, while less physical than the rescue, took a heavy toll on all aboard. More tears were shed that day than any of the days prior, and you understood the cost of all of this.

The Feeding Grounds. The places or walks of life we choose that deep down we know aren't good for us. They will kill us. Maybe not take our life, but a part of us can die. We can't seem to break free from the grasp these things have on us. Addiction is a monster of the deep that lives in this place. When you start down the road of researching addiction, you'll find there are many disagreements on the exact specifics related to it. Addiction's categorization as a disease fit with some models, but the extensive unknowns related to the brain suggest many counter arguments. All generally agree it involves the compulsive seeking and taking of a substance or performing an activity, chasing some perceived or felt benefit despite negative or harmful consequences.

Regardless of terminology—disease, stronghold, sin pattern—the impact is real, and hope remains the same for any in the dark waters of the feeding grounds.

Where the addiction tends to be masked for many is that you are participating in an activity that millions of other people partake in with no issues at all, but you don't realize that you are doing it differently than everyone else.

"There is a way that appears to be right, but in the end it leads to death." Proverbs 14:12

Some statistics say that about one in three individuals suffer from some sort of addiction. I'm not a huge fan of statistics because if I've learned anything from one college-level, basic statistics course it is that any data can be used to say about whatever you want. This isn't to downplay this statistic, but I lean more into the camp that it is more likely that two-thirds of people haven't found the thing they are addicted to. Because it isn't like the science of addiction doesn't apply to two-thirds of people. They just haven't found the thing that produces similar levels of dopamine to dump, causing a rewiring in the brain to seek out that same feeling again. Since our creation, we have been pretty good at understanding what actions create that feeling and we repeat them again and again.

With the invention of the modern cellular device, I would further argue against the only one in three number. I think many people are addicted to their devices, and it has become an acceptable norm in society. There are a number of things in modern life that are supported or even praised as being acceptable. Binge drinking, you need help; binging four seasons of a Netflix show in a week, you are a huge fan. I'm sure you could identify several other addictions that are generally accepted by society today.

But counter-tech rants, productivity, and efficiency aren't what this chapter is about. It is about us living in these places, these feeding grounds. Why do we live there? Yes, we are chasing a dopamine dump, but why do we choose to live there? Why do we choose to return to the place or places we know we shouldn't? Why do we believe we have it all under control and won't get pulled under by the beast, dragged back to the depths?

Spend some time answering those questions. Name your feeding ground. Write it down. Then name the first step toward surfacing again. Surfacing back to everything God created you to be. Because He sees you for everything beautiful you truly are, and although you may be dwelling in this place now, there is a hope to leave that all behind you. We just need to take the first step and get back out of the water.

The Fog

On the way from the Feeding Grounds to home harbor, you encountered a curious anomaly. The fog crept in like a silent tide, swallowing sight and sound, leaving an eerie feeling throughout the ship. The warm air swirled about, meeting the cold water below and causing white clouds to form. What was known ahead on the water melted away behind the sheer density of the white wall.

You call for the ship to slow and sound the bell every two minutes. The rest of the crew, knowing their jobs, light lamps around the ship to give your location to any other ships limping their way through the fog. The bell—your only voice in the void—rang out into nothing.

Knowing where you're heading as the fog settles helps, but the rocky outcroppings along the route may prove deadly if the white wall doesn't lift. At this speed you feel you could sail for some time before arriving to those dangerous waters.

You remind the crew, "Remember eyes and ears all! Even if you think you may have seen or heard something relay it on. It could save the ship and all those on it."

You continue sailing on your heading. The silence of the crew is almost as eerie as the white fog engulfing every bit of the ship.

"HARD TO PORT, BOOM AGAINST THE WIND!" the voice rings out.

Without question, you spin the wheel as far to the left as it will go. You hear the rest of the crew pushing the mainsail against the wind and hope that there won't be a sudden smashing of rock against wood.

You squint into the mist, looking for any sign of the thing the ship was trying to avoid.

The ship stops hard as the sail catches the wind the opposite way. The crew hoists it as to not back into whatever was avoided.

"I heard a bell, off our bow on the starboard side, Captain," Quincy says as he appears out of the fog nearby. "Tom told me to come, let you know."

"That's a good lad, Quince... how far?" you ask.

"I'm not sure, Captain, but knew I had to say something," Quincy says, sure of what he heard.

"Thank you, Quincy. You can head back."

You let Quincy disappear into the ether before turning the wheel back to center in frustration. You listen, straining to hear a bell or any sound that may give any new information, knowing that with that maneuver your bearing was lost and you'll have to wait for the fog to clear before you could set full sail again.

"Throw the lead line!" you shout, asking for a depth check. Should be more than 100 fathoms based on the course.

"Throwing the lead line!" one of the crew shouts back through the fog.

A few moments pass.

"Seven fathoms!" the voice calls out giving the depth.

"Seventy?" you question in earnest.

"Seven!" the voice comes back.

Forty-two feet! you think. *How is the boat in forty-two feet of water. It should be well over five-hundred feet of water.* Your stomach drops. This wasn't just fog—it was disorientation. You aren't where you thought you were.

Tom appears out of the abyss, matching the look of shock on your face.

"How'd that happen?" Tom asks.

"Got me. May as well anchor at this depth and sound the bell until it clears," you reply.

Tom hurries off to give the orders, and you hear the ship preparing to settle in until the fog clears, the anchor dropping into the water and the chain following after it.

The crew moves about the ship slower than normal as to not collide with each other as they carry out their normal tasks.

You take this time to peer into the mist off the bow and stern, trying to make out any semblance of a course. Not even the sun shines through well enough in the canopy to tell a location, and you resign to wait it out.

The whole day passes into the night and the fog continues to linger around the ship.

"Have you ever seen it last this long?" Tom asks, bringing you a cup of coffee to the helm.

"No, it's strange," you say as you take the coffee and attempt to blow the heat off the top layer before taking a sip.

"The sun will burn through it in the morning," Tom says, drinking his own coffee.

"I don't know. It could be something else…" You drift off a bit not wanting to say, *It came on quick and thick, lingering like no fog I've seen.*

Tom eyes you for a moment, knowing what you are thinking.

"If it is… that, we should pull anchor and crawl out of here. Better to do that than wait. We could be in here ages before it lifts."

You blow on the coffee again, staring at the mist through the steam off the cup, taking another sip.

"We probably shou…" You pause, listening for something behind you off the back of the ship. "Did you hear that?"

You turn and walk to the stern; Tom follows.

"I don't think so," Tom says. "You may be hearing things at this point."

You close your eyes, straining to hear off the back of the ship, trying to shut off all other senses. You know you heard something.

"It was there. I know it," you say.

Tom strains along with you, trying to hear what you say you heard.

The time slips by as you listen and when both of you almost give up hope. As clear as can be, a bell sounds off in the distance off the back of the ship.

Tom runs over to the deck bell and rings twice in response.

The bell in the distance sounds again.

As if echo-locating each other, Tom and the mystery bell respond in kind, with the distant bell closing the gap, getting closer and closer to the ship.

A faint glow pierces the mist long before the sound of their hull against the water reaches your ears. A small skiff approaches, coming alongside the ship.

"They told me there was a ship out here in the middle of this," the scruffy looking skiff captain hollers up jovially. "Can I help you pilot her out?"

"You know the way out of this?" you ask.

"I do. I do. Of course, I'll need the help of yourself and your crew. I'm just the guide. Permission to come aboard?" he asks with a kindness in his voice.

You look over to Tom, asking what he thinks without speaking a word. Tom shrugs in response to your silent question.

"Permission granted. What should we call you?" you ask, and he is already making his way up a rope and onto your ship.

He waves at his crew on the skiff as they push off and disappear into the mist the same as they arrived.

"Captain George is the name," he says, shaking anyone's hand that is around you. "Now shall we get you out of this fog?"

"Absolutely," you say in response.

Captain George wastes no time as he starts explaining what is going to happen from the next few moments into the next thirty or forty minutes. He explains what he needs from you and Tom and then moves on to other members of the crew based on the jobs they held. Everything from heading, speed, sail trim, weight placement around the ship, and much more. It seems so granular, but the way he explains it makes perfect sense, and no one questions the directions.

As you get underway, Captain George stands right beside you as you pilot the ship. He hollers out instructions as needed and corrects your directions at times.

He stares into the fog like it is nothing to him, like he can see right through it and all the ocean before him.

"Where were y'all headed before you stopped to help?" you ask as you continue to pilot the ship.

"Oh." He chuckles a bit. "Here, this is what we do. The fog comes up on ships faster than they know what to do, get turned around sailing in circles, close to rocks at times. If they're lucky, they don't hit 'em, and they end up stopping like y'all. We sail out here to get them going again."

"How do you know the way through?" you ask.

He smiles, loving to share this part.

"I lived in it for years. It's not just above the water you know. It exists below, a thick cloud of silt and debris. It affects us all above and below, and I lived in it in both. Until one day I decided to move forward. I moved all through the fog, trying to find the way out of it. I couldn't, not until someone like me sailed up in it and told me all the things I've told you. He helped me pilot my way out of it, taught me how to help others do the same. And now, I do that job."

You smile. "A noble purpose."

"Indeed," he replies.

"Can you even see the fog?" you ask.

"Oh, I see it all right. I just recognize it for what it is, and that's what helps clear it up for me," he says.

"What is it?" you ask. "It came up out of nowhere."

He taps a finger on the side of his nose.

"It is the overwhelming and all-consuming nature of life. Sometimes the smallest distraction brings the fog that causes us to lose our way. While with others, it is a force that reorders our complete world in the most terrible way, and we can't see inches in front of our face," he replies.

"Without our bearings, we couldn't move. Too much was at stake," you state.

"There is most assuredly a time to pause, rest, recover, but never stop. I've come upon ships that are frozen in time, those who stopped and didn't make it," he says, taking in a deep breath, remembering those challenging encounters.

"Thankfully, that doesn't appear to be your fate." He says pointing toward the horizon.

The sun peaks through the mist ahead for the first time in a long time.

"Keep this heading, and you'll be all the way out in no time. I gotta catch my ship," he says over his shoulder as he walks toward the side of the ship he boarded on.

"Wait... should we slow?" you yell after him.

"Are you kidding? This is the fun part," he says as he eyes the mist.

Out of nowhere, his skiff appears, racing alongside the ship. As it approaches, he gives one big wave and swings on a rope across the void between ships, landing on the deck toward the front of the skiff.

"Thank you!" you holler after him.

His crew waves and turns back into the fog, looking for another ship to help.

The fog continues to melt away, not all at once as it arose, but fast enough to get bearings and settle back on course.

"Remind me to send them a proper thank you," you tell Tom as he stands by your side.

The rest of the journey to home harbor is without note, peaceful even. Your time with the crew and those pulled from the water is memorable, even given the circumstances surrounding the Feeding Grounds. You're glad to be returning to the ship build and hope the team has made good progress, even without you there, but you can't get Charlie's comments out of your head, the hurt in his voice. You wish you could have talked to him longer, but something in you knows it won't be the last time you see him.

Sailing blind, while the actions of sailing are the same, the feeling is entirely different. Blindness coupled with losing your bearing is the worst of situations. You have no ability to regain your bearings since your fixed points have disappeared. In life, this can occur with the loss of a loved one, the fixed point with which everything seemed to make sense. To have a fixed plan and bearing in life vanish in a fog with no idea when it will lift or which way you are going, not knowing if you are on the right path or making all the wrong choices while also dealing with this new way of life is frightening.

Our story's change isn't permanent. It is an unknown fog that halted the fixed plan. It could be anything in your life that causes this. Hopefully it isn't anything as tragic as the loss of a spouse or child. Sometimes fog isn't failure—it's transition. It could be a forced career change, a move, a series of good decisions that brought you to a place of more choices than you know what to do with and those things become a wall of unclarity.

When you experience this type of fog, slowing the boat is a viable option. Stopping has its place; anchoring has its place. Proverbs 3:5-6 says, "Trust in the Lord with all your heart and lean not on your own understanding; in all your ways submit to him, and he will make your paths straight." Whatever decision you make about navigating the fog it is clear that trusting in the Lord is step number one. Too often we try to reason ourselves through a storm instead of leaning on Him.

Whether a health fog, a career fog, or an emotional fog, how it presents for you can be in a myriad of ways, but stopping to evaluate is never a bad idea on the front end. Sometimes the fog will clear on its own, and it was just one of those weird instances we all experience. In others, the fog lingers, and careening ahead at full speed can cause serious damage to yourself and all around. Stopping and reevaluating is a great step before moving forward again.

Once you've experienced this fog and dealt with it firsthand, you become a prime candidate to help others navigate it. Captain George, in our story, had lived in the fog for years, and when someone helped him out of it, they taught him the tools and insight to help others make their way through the fog. Your light gets a little bit brighter, and your bell sounds a little bit louder as you journey through the fog looking for those who are lost.

Once you've escaped the fog, keep an eye out for others who are in it. You'll know the signs now that you've been in it yourself. Ask them if they'll let you help them pilot out of it. Ask permission to come aboard. Don't do it for them, but walk beside them and help them do it for themselves. Be their Captain George.

THE SIRENS

The fire crackled low in The Retreat's hearth as the old man's voice broke the hush.

"Have I ever told you the tale of the Sisyphean Sirens?" the old man asks to nobody in particular as he stares into the fireplace of The Retreat.

Upon your return, you found the ship build on track for delivery, the team working together better than you could have hoped. You and Tom fell right back into the usual routine of working sunup to sunset with a stop off at The Retreat before doing it all over again. Stories were often told till the late hours, and this was no different.

"No, I don't think so," you oblige to answer even though you aren't sure if he was talking to you.

"The Sisyphean shores are due south, maybe a month's journey if you have the wind the whole way. We were sent to recover and resupply a stranded vessel that had run aground along the shores. How it wasn't dashed to pieces, we weren't sure. The rocks there are all black and volcanic; the jagged edges could cut through your hull like that butter there."

He points the knife he's holding at the butter on your table, out of reach. You push it closer, and he swipes a tab off the stick, wipes it onto a roll, then devours it.

"We had rough coordinates for where the ship was, but upon eyeing the shoreline, the captain kept a wide berth and sailed up the shore glassing for the ship."

He washes the roll down with another drink.

"The cold was the first thing you notice with the sirens, as if they themselves dropped the water temperature. We all felt it, but I was the first to see. Cold fingers swirled through the water moving toward the surface.... Playfully pulling at the water. The water parted for them as it did for others, but something about this was different and foreign. The fingers surfaced first and then the head of a creature... The sirens. First one and then another surfaced. You see some of them had been pulled from the water, and not liking the savior's song, retreated back below. Soon what looked like hundreds were above and below the surface all around the ship. The lack of sound was alarming for how many were there now, not even a breath could be heard from them as they watched the ship, waiting."

He watched the fire and got closer, as if the chill of the story itself was overcoming him.

"The song, I can still hear it. Beautiful, but... the words, wrong, they were. *You deserve, you earned, you are perfect, they owe you*... the melody wrapped around our minds like a warm lie. Each word stroking ego." He pauses.

Pulling a small piece of silver out of his pocket, he begins rolling it across his fingers without looking away from the fire.

"Good to hear, but it wasn't right. The tone, the intonation itself was angry, almost bitter. It filled the air, and you could almost taste it. One chorus after another the same thing. Focusing on it was all you could do; we almost didn't see our ship heading for the rocks."

He holds the coin up, letting the light shine and shimmer on its surface.

"Like the siren's praise, shiny and precious—until tested," he says.

He slams the coin onto the table and brings the knife tip down into the middle of it. The knife pierces the coin with no resistance, showing its true nature, counterfeit, brittle.

"That's all those voices were, empty, baseless, sycophantic, saying only the things the listener wanted to hear. We countered the song as we worked to save the ship and our lives. We sang what we knew was lovely and true."

He pauses staring again into the fire.

"What happened?" you ask, leaning into the story.

"Well, those sirens didn't like that one bit. Every word we sang was counter to their core beliefs, which were that we were the ones to be praised, to be validated, to be accepted, and honored as we were. We sang louder than they ever could, drowning out the lies of their song. They threw themselves against our ship but couldn't do any real damage."

He tosses the fake coin into the fire, watching the façade melt away.

"They sank back into the depths," he whispers. "They're called Sisyphean, not because of who the sirens were—but because of what they offered: promises that never delivered."

No one spoke for a long while.

"Is it possible to change a siren's song, bring them back to living on the surface?" you finally ask.

"Anything is possible. I don't know that I've seen it, but it requires them to reject their very being, their core, everything that has sustained them to that moment they reject as untrue and choose truth, but"—he pauses as he sits a little further back in his chair—"that would be a thing to see... and hear. All those beautiful voices in proper chorus with the truth. One day maybe," he says as he gets lost again in the fire.

"One day," you echo.

What songs do you sing to yourself, or allow others to sing to you? What truths might you be avoiding while tuning in to lies that feel more comfortable? Romans 16:17-18 says, "I urge you, brothers and sisters, to watch out for those who cause divisions and put obstacles in your way that are contrary to the teaching you have learned. Keep away from them. For such people are not serving our Lord Christ, but their own appetites. By smooth talk and flattery they deceive the minds of naïve people."

We all could take an hour listing out the things in our life that we've decided to believe about either ourselves, or our situation, or others, or the world. Things we've been told or things we've simply decided to believe. Whatever it may be, the siren's song in our lives is a perversion of the truth. Truth twisted with lies, almost impossible to see where the truth ends and the lie begins.

For most that song of lies is much easier to listen to than the truth. *I can't buy a house because the economy is in the gutter. I can't find a spouse because there aren't any good options out there. I didn't get the promotion because of office politics.* The trick to a siren's song is to weave enough truth in with it to make you think it is all truth, but the roots of the song are all lies.

The housing market can be difficult to get into for a single individual starting out.

Finding a spouse can be super tricky in many different situations.

Office politics can be a thing, and your workplace could be a mine field.

But also...

What are *your* home expectations, and have *you* created a solid financial plan so *you* can buy a house?

Where are *you* looking for a future partner? What are *you* doing to make yourself that dream spouse?

What could *you* have done to earn the promotion? If it is a bad situation, why aren't *you* looking to exit?

We like to listen to the siren's song because it sounds better to us in the moment, but that type of thinking will leave us shattered upon the shore. We'll live in a place where we never do the hard work because it is always someone or something's fault. Never our own.

Recognize that as soon as we start filling our ears with songs and words of truth, we'll sing that to others as well. Truth multiplies. One voice speaks it; another picks it up. And before long, the song of the sirens is drowned out by a greater chorus—one that heals, restores, and awakens.

What siren's song are you going to stop listening to today? We all have one. What is yours?

If you hold to my teaching, you are really my disciples. Then you will know the truth, and the truth will set you free.

John 8:31-32

Hitting a Wall

"Tom!" you call out into the dark hull.

"Hey, I'm here. I'm here," Tom calls back out of the darkness.

A dim light turns a corner down the length of the ship and starts moving toward you. Tom's silhouette takes shape as it gets closer. It's obvious he has been sleeping.

"Everything good?" you ask, already knowing something wasn't.

"Yeah, yeah, all good. Just taking a break," Tom retorts.

"Tom, it's me. Can we skip the part where we waste two hours pretending something's not wrong? Is it her?" You pause to try and see if there is any response.

Tom, annoyed, pushes past you out of the ship.

"Because if it is, I want you to go find her," you finish, still waiting to catch a response as you follow him out of the ship into the shipyard.

Tom blows his lantern out and sets it by several others. Looking up at the sky, he closes his eyes and takes a deep breath in and out.

"No... it isn't her. I don't think... I don't know... We make these decisions about how we're going to live and what we're going to do with the time that we have, and you get to these points where it's like you've suddenly woken up on a ship that's already halfway across the sea. You're sailing, but you can't remember why. Is this what I chose? Is this where I'm at, and what I'll be doing the next five, ten, twenty years?" Tom pauses, realizing his words could be sharp if taken the wrong way.

You hold up a hand, seeing Tom's worried face.

"Tom, I get it. I get feeling lost in the moment. Doubting the choices you've made, that you continue to make. You've been with me since the beginning, and

I know I'm blessed by having you around, but if you have to go, if it's something you need, know I want that for you."

Tom takes in your words and looks over the bay. Several ships sail out, and a few sail in.

"I don't even remember asking myself what it was that I wanted. I'm sure I thought about it, but I can't remember why I decided what I did. And now I'm here helping build this giant ship, and it's never going to end."

You chuckle at the thought.

"What's so funny?" Tom asks.

"I've thought the exact same thing."

"It's not the same for you. It is your commission. This is what you are supposed to be doing. You have a piece of paper that says it."

Tom sits on the edge of the jetty outside the berth.

"I mean, I'll get you a piece of paper if that's what you want," you joke.

Tom, not amused, lets you know it.

"You don't get it though. Everything we've done has been what you were supposed to be doing. And I helped sure, but"—Tom starts getting to the real heart of the issue—"am I not special enough to a get a commission of my own?"

You sit down next to him, realizing that his statement is the heart of the problem at hand.

"Tom, I couldn't have completed any of my commissions without you. They don't have your name on them, but you were right there helping to save people. My success was your success, my failures; you've taken them on right by my side."

Tom thinks on it while watching the ships.

"I was sleeping back there because lately it is the only way I can turn my brain off. I can't seem to shake all this. I know the truth, but even when you say it, when I say it, I don't believe it. I'm left with nothing."

You're at a loss for words at this point. You've unloaded both barrels of encouragement and nothing has helped.

As if summoned by the conversation itself, the Harbormaster squeezes in and sits down right between you handing you each a cup.

"You mind if I join?" the Harbormaster asks, already sitting.

He pours the liquid into each of your cups and then His own. He caps the bottle and then sips on His own cup.

"Have you two ever heard the story of the three captains?" The Harbormaster looks to you and then to Tom. "I didn't think so. It's an older one."

He proceeds to tell the story:

Three captains sat in the harbor staring at each of their ships. Each captain was adorned with medals and honors that had been bestowed upon them from all around.

"My ship is the fastest ship in the harbor," the first captain stated pointing to his large ship in the harbor.

The other captains scoffed together.

The second captain stepped forward pointing to another grand vessel anchored. "You see my ship right there; my ship is faster than all the ships on this sea."

Both captains are offended by this statement, but the third captain pushes through.

"My ship, the largest and mightiest in the harbor, is the fastest ship in the whole world."

All three captains begin arguing among themselves and never notice a young girl listening to them.

The young girl looks over the ships, using her telescope to inspect them. After surveying each of the ships, she turns to the group.

"I'll wager my boat is faster than all of yours!"

The three captains look at the young girl and laugh it off, but soon realize she isn't kidding as she sits there and stares at them.

"Child, your ship surely can't keep up with any of our ships," the first captain says.

The girl looks over their ships again.

"I'll race any one of your ships right now," she says.

"Our sails are being repaired from the storms; we can't race," the second captain says.

The young girl smiles at the three captains.

"Then at this moment, right now, mine is the fastest ship in the harbor, this sea, and possibly the world."

The young girl departs down to the shore where she boards her small dinghy and sails out into the harbor, sailing circles around all three boats before setting out to sea.

The captains all watched and smiled as they realized the importance of her little lesson.

Tom stares into the ocean watching the waves crash in, never ceasing.

"No offense, sir, but I don't know what this has to do with anything," Tom states, never breaking eye contact with the water.

The Harbormaster sips on His drink and thinks for a moment.

"What does it mean for you?"

Tom thinks for a moment. "They are stuck, so they shouldn't be bragging about how great their ships are."

The Harbormaster smiles. "Sure, sure, face value, that is part of the story. Having the humility to recognize their current limitations, but that's what I love about these stories, so many other aspects. Each captain saw the full potential of the gift they'd been given. They shouldn't have been arguing about it, but alas, they're human. Each one saw their ship, their commission as the very best."

"What if you don't have a commission?" Tom asks.

"Who ever said you needed a ship or a piece of paper to have a commission? What about when you know in your heart of hearts the thing you were doing was right and good and had purpose? Or knowing when it is time to push on to something else? People often forget that; they sit around waiting for some grand sign to tell them what to do and blame the lack of a sign for all the ills in their life. True, life change is many times a single decision away, but they don't do it," the Harbormaster says as He peers into His cup, wishing there was more.

"So how do we know?" you ask.

"Ask yourself if what you're doing is true, noble, right... if it's pure, lovely, admirable, excellent and praiseworthy. Commit that list to memory. Focus on those things like they matter, because they do. And then the real secret is"—He leans in close as if to give away some great mystery of the universe—"you live!"

He shouts, amused at Himself. "Do the next right thing, and if you aren't sure what that is. Think on that list and I bet you can figure it out. It may not be the perfect choice, but I know it'll never be the wrong one."

We all hit a wall at some point—emotionally, spiritually, circumstantially. Sometimes it's frustration that ran us into it. Other times it's grief or burnout. We don't discuss it as often as we should because I think we are ashamed of being unhappy with the current state of our situation.

In the Bible, Job has choice words for God about losing nearly everything he held dear, but we struggle with all forms of loss and how to grieve it. One of the lowest points in my life, like clinically depressed lows, included a series of events where the outcomes weren't in my favor. They weren't losses by anyone else's standards, but I attributed them as a loss because what I was hoping for didn't work out. I did all the work and couldn't get what I felt was a single win.

People say things like, "Shoot for the moon, and if you miss, you'll still be among the stars." I don't like it; it doesn't bring comfort to the person who took their shot and are now bankrupt and broken. I understand the sentiment, and I agree that failing is a form of education that can be necessary to growth, but that doesn't make it feel any better when it happens.

In this story, the wall Tom hits is one of personal accomplishment or a lack of feeling any. The thought that creeps in on Tom is that he hasn't accomplished anything, and all the advancement belongs to you. This idea creeps in at different stages through life. I've noticed a large number of younger people, early twenties to thirties, who say things like, "I do all the work, and they make all the money."

I felt that way for about 2.3 seconds while working for a veterinarian in college. Once I learned, what I thought was a great deal of the job, I was trusted to carry out much of the work independently, and I understand why people get it in their head to feel this way. As a skilled worker, you provide a great deal of effort for the organization, but my 2.3 second moment of critical thinking led me to recognize my work paled in comparison to the insurmountable amount that the doctor and his wife had put into the clinic. Not only the schooling required and the licenses on the wall, but the countless hours building a client list who loved and trusted them. I had too much evidence of the doc's hard work, dedication, and literal scars from caring for sick animals—who were scared and kicked, bit, slammed—to let those thoughts linger too long. I recognized I played a role in *his* business—not my own—and was compensated fairly for it. Even though that was the case, it didn't mean my hard work was worthless. I was a trusted employee who received way more than a paycheck from the doc and his wife.

Tom is in a hard place. You may know the feeling—watching others receive affirmation, the praise, while wondering if your work matters. I think we all can get to a place very similar to Tom if we aren't careful. We forget the most important part of it all, our why.

"Let us not become weary in doing good," Paul writes in Galatians 6:9, "for at the proper time we will reap a harvest if we do not give up."

That verse isn't a promise of instant clarity or praise, but it is a lifeline when we're weary and unsure if what we're doing still matters. Tom had forgotten his why. He attributed his pain to a lack of any personal commission but had forgotten why he started sailing with you in the first place.

The Harbormaster offered some great advice about not needing a commission to feel accomplished in the day to day, living out your own personal mission absent a piece of paper. But that may not be where you are at yet. You may feel lost, like Tom, in the current state of life, unsure where you are going or what you are doing and questioning the worth of the decisions you've made that brought you here.

Getting back to your original why is key. We've discussed it already in different ways, but it really is at the crux of so many aspects of this journey on the surface. Take some time to reexamine your why behind it all. You may find it is right there where you left it and you just hadn't thought about it recently, or you may find you have been living an old why and need to reposition yourself. It is important that we do this work of evaluating the why so that we can grow and move into the person we are supposed to be: the best version of ourselves that God wishes for each and every one of us.

THE CHRISTENING

The christening ceremony for the ship was the largest you've seen since you've arrived at the harbor years ago. People filled the harbor, shoulder to shoulder on every dock, lining balconies, even standing on anchored skiffs. The crowds—most people you recognize, but many you don't—came from all over, some by boat just to be a part of the launching of this huge ship.

You stand with your small crew that built her from the ground up, proud of everything you've accomplished together.

The last few evenings, as work would finish, the conversations had shifted to everyone's plans after this day. Several hoped to have a place among its crew, looking to you for confirmation.

"Don't look at me. It may not be mine to captain," you said with a peace you'd already achieved having thought about that potential outcome long before the conversation.

Everyone looked at you, baffled that you would think that.

"What do you mean?" several said in their own way.

"The commission was clear—build it, finish by this date. Nothing about captaining it after. I've read over that commission many times, and I made peace with that. Whether it is me or someone else, I'm sure it'll be the right person for the job. Harbormaster knows what He is doing."

They all sat with that information.

"But we are going out on her at least once, right? Maiden voyage?" Tom asked hoping.

You mulled it over for a moment.

"I mean we have to, right?"

Everyone smiled at the thought.

Now the day has come, and the ship is ready to be named.

Everyone waits for the Harbormaster to come.

Before long, a small procession can be seen moving down the street toward that end of the harbor. The Harbormaster and His large stature can't be missed moving in the middle of the group.

As they get closer, you can see someone is walking with Him. An older man, a captain by the look of him. Sea worn and steady.

The Harbormaster walks toward you and your small team.

"What you all have accomplished brings me great joy. Truly a sight to see." The Harbormaster beams with joy.

The words will mean more to your crew than anything else for quite some time.

The Harbormaster looks to you.

"Thank you for your diligence and leadership in building this vessel," He says.

"It was an honor, sir," you reply.

"Let me introduce you to Captain Levi. He'll be captaining the ship for the time being."

Even having made your peace with it, hearing the words still doesn't feel great, but regardless, you smile and greet the ship's new captain.

"It is a pleasure, sir. I think I've heard of your work in the southern seas," you say finding the name familiar.

"Yes, we'd been there quite some time and got the word we were needed up here, so here I am," he replies.

"Well, shall we?" the Harbormaster says.

The ceremony goes like most before it. The Harbormaster says a few words about the importance of the mission and how each of those there are a critical part of it. The ship's naming is next.

"And for the name," the Harbormaster says.

The drape covering the name and figurehead is pulled away, revealing a beautiful carving of a man throwing a net into the water below. A hush falls, then cheers ripple out like a wave.

"*Kenosis*," the crowd yells in delight.

"To empty," Tom says to the team as a few of their faces show they'd never heard the word.

"I like it," the team responds. "Yeah me too. The ship that'll empty the seas."

You nod your approval while thinking about another meaning.

During the tour with Captain Levi and the crew that came with him, you have a few moments alone with Captain Levi while the rest of your team shows everyone around.

"The name is fitting," he says as you walk together along the main deck. The Harbormaster not far behind listening in.

"I agree," you say. "I hope it does that to the sea, empties it of all the people it can. But also, I like the idea that it takes one emptying themselves to do this work. Less of me."

Captain Levi stops along the railing looking out of the harbor at the sea.

"I couldn't agree more. The very heart of the mission. Not power, but surrender. Many sacrifices have been made to live this life, but in the end, I can't remember them compared to the change I've witnessed. How everything works exactly how it was intended to. That when we listen and obey, we end up being where we are supposed to be."

The words bring a warmth to your heart, and you realize Captain Levi is the right person to take the ship out and you are happy for it.

"If it isn't too much to ask," Captain Levi starts again. "Would you join me on this first mission? You and any of the team that built her. It would be an immense favor, helping us, since you know this ship backward and forward."

You think on it for a moment. The offer is the best of both worlds. Seeing what the ship can do, but also the removal of the burden of leadership.

"I'm in. I know several of the team would love to join as well," you respond.

"Great news!" the Harbormaster says, listening in to every word. "This is going to be a great commission."

The Harbormaster hands the papers to Captain Levi, who reads them over.

You wait—just long enough to imagine him offering the paper to you. Instead, he turns, his brow furrowed, rushing to his first mate.

The Harbormaster puts His hand on your shoulder.

"You don't have to worry about that part now," He says, giving a reassuring squeeze.

"I don't know if I know how to not worry about that part," you say.

The Harbormaster smiles.

"You'll love it. One focus, getting to make that one thing the main thing. You'll be right at home in no time."

With another squeeze, the Harbormaster moves on to others around the ship, encouraging and giving words of wisdom as He goes. You lean on the rail to watch the ocean.

"I hear we're sailing?" Tom says from behind you.

"Word travels fast. Yes, anyone from the team is welcome to join," you respond as you turn to him.

He joins you at the rail.

"You decide if you are sticking around or moving on?" you ask, having not broached the subject since the conversation at the harbor.

Tom looks at the ocean, thinking for moment.

"Something tells me, just one more," he says, watching the water.

"Just one more," you say clasping his shoulder, both staring out to sea. "Let's make it a good one."

Relinquishing control of something you've built with your own two hands is one of the most challenging things to do. An aging founder and CEO passing their company on, a pastor stepping away from a congregation they helped plant, or a child watching their younger sibling play with a model they built, the feelings can all be the same.

You've invested part of yourself into the success or completion of this thing, and the last thing you want to see is it destroyed by someone else who doesn't care for it the way you do.

But that itself is a fallacy in assuming that someone else could not care the same amount or even more than you do.

In our story, you have already wrestled with the possibility that this thing you were called to build may not be best captained with you at the helm. For many people, this takes quite some time to get to that place of relinquishment.

Parents with teenage children, preparing to leave the nest, as they say, will know this firsthand. You watch your children grow, working to shape them and teach them all the things you wish you had been taught. You love them the way you believe they should be loved. Then you watch them fly, cringing at the places they decide to go, cheering when they take off to the places you'd hoped for them, but letting them go off on their own.

Oddly enough, I once heard a line in the 1997 film, *Starship Troopers* that's stuck with me ever since. Johnny Rico, the main character, and his platoon have lost their leader, and they need a new one. When Rico is offered the job he responds, "I'll take it, till I get killed or you find someone better."

Since the first time I heard it, it struck me as such a mature concept. When I know the thing is bigger than myself, is bigger than anyone else, I know A.) I'll give it my all even if it kills me and B.) I'll step aside for someone better and more capable than myself to help this thing succeed.

Maturity is recognizing we may not always be the one to take the baton across the finish line—nor do we want to be—when we know there is someone else better positioned and/or equipped to do it. First Corinthians 3:6 says, "I planted the seed, Apollos watered it, but God has been making it grow." We won't always be there from start to finish, nor should we be. We are called for a purpose, and we should be willing, but we also must recognize when to relinquish control so that someone better equipped to water can come and do the next step of the work, better than you can. It is about the mission first and foremost. A mission bigger than you and I. A calling bigger than you and I. In these moments, we work to remember to set our egos aside. The mission is too important to make it about us. If I can save only one, it'll be worth it. Kenosis—that's the call. To empty. Till I die... or He finds someone better.

The Mission to the Golden Harbor

The crisp early morning air was so much better on the water. The first few days of sailing had been interesting to say the least. Nothing wrong with the ship, but a rhythm had to be found among the crew. The way specific aspects of the boats design functioned in the water were new to everyone, including your team who built it. It all functioned as expected but took a little bit for everyone to get used to. The ships unique design—especially the multiple bilge keels—created unfamiliar drag at low speeds, which at first felt like something was wrong. It took several maneuvers for everyone to feel the drag and realize that that was what was causing the slower starts.

You had been assigned as an advisor on the ship, while Tom was given a more specific assignment managing the cargo holds and ensuring proper rationing was occurring.

As advisor, you met with the captain once a day, more if needed, answered any questions that had arisen during the day's sailing, and provided thoughts overall on how to best utilize the ships tools.

"We have about ten more days of sailing before we reach the keys," Captain Levi says. "I know that is a lot of time, but I'd like to go over some contingencies with the ship before we get there and give the crew plenty of time to understand what they will do in any given situation."

"That's wise," you reply, watching Captain Levi lay out two maps of the keys, one an overall map covering all of them, then another with the specific key the ship will be visiting. "What is that?" you ask pointing at a large golden circle on the map.

"The Golden Harbor," Captain Levi responds, placing another map of the harbor down over the top of it. "Hopefully, where we will be docking, but reporting indicates it may be closed. I want to have a plan about how to approach if that is the case. There may be other issues as well that we'll need to discuss."

"Like what?" you ask.

Captain Levi looks over the map, not thinking about the question.

"Cannons. Several cannons," the first mate, Oliver, responds for him.

"It's been years since I've been there so I'm trying to decide if I were to place cannons there, where I would put them?"

Captain Levi places several small circles around the outer edge of the harbor. Oliver points to one more area, and another circle is added.

"Yes, probably," Captain Levi says.

Cannons had never crossed your mind. You'd seen what they had done to other ships, but now the thought of this ship facing them was a bit too much.

"Several? You know this ship wasn't built to withstand any of that? Unless, of course, it was shooting the bottom of the ship, but last time I checked, cannons don't work like that." Your frustration in just now being told about this part of the mission shines through.

"It shouldn't be anything for us to worry about. We'll either be outside of their range or someplace they can't hit us." Captain Levi looks you in the eyes with a calmness and confidence. "We will prepare, but I need you to trust me when I tell you I would never place you or your people in the way of harm you weren't prepared to address."

You pause, taking in the words.

"I believe you. I don't know why a harbor like that would ever need such a thing," you respond.

"They never had them while I was there. In fact, we welcomed the challenges, the little attacks, because it told us that what we were doing was being noticed for all the right reasons. The Harbormaster's plans tend to do that. But then something changed. I don't know if they became tired of it, or they really feel threatened, but they started fighting fire with fire and ended up where they are. Walled-in, away from it all. No more ships coming in or out. Willing to fire on any who approach." Captain Levi pulls back from the map having drawn several intersecting lines with potential paths through lines of fire.

"This path is our best chance, but we'll have to come in hot and be ready to drop the anchor and stop quick. That or the rocks will stop us quick."

You smile at that. "I know the bottom can take a hit, that I'm sure of."

"Let's pray it doesn't have to," Captain Levi says, looking over the single safe path to the harbor.

The three of you look at the path, recognizing how precise a maneuver it'll have to be.

"Oliver, based on this path, time, and distance at max speed, can you prepare drills for the crew? I want them to be prepared." Captain Levi hands the map to Oliver.

"Aye, aye, Captain." Oliver takes the map and returns to his cabin to make the drill plans.

Turning to you, Captain Levi looks you in the eyes. "I need you to talk to your people. Encourage them. Spread hope. The idea of cannons won't be easy for those who haven't encountered them before."

"Aye, Captain. Will do," you say as you get up and exit.

The days passed and it has been hard on the crew. The drills are stringent and the path precise. The first drills required the crew to understand how to get the ship to accomplish the maneuvers. Shaping into the turns, what speed would be lost, and how to regain it to keep on the path. While Captain Levi maintained every bit of control through the turns, he needed to understand where the wheel had to be prior to taking it there, and the practice was a necessity for all. At the end of it, the crew understood what needed to happen and when. Oliver maintained a sand timer and called out maneuvers, but once trained, they knew the timing by heart.

The day came, and off in the far distance, the whole crew could see the shining glimmer that was the Golden Harbor. Truly beautiful, the sun shone off the gold that plated most of the buildings. Captain Levi viewed it through a spyglass.

"You all know what you have to do. What we are here to do. When we get to the wall, I will speak. Don't engage with them. That is why I am here. Stay the course." Captain Levi steps to the helm.

Oliver takes over the commands, preparing everyone to start the maneuvers. The next fifteen minutes fly by like the cannon balls challenging our approach.

With the plan set, the ship reaches maximum speed hurtling toward the first turn. The moment the ship began the turn, the cannons sound, two at first and another three firing at the previous course.

The cannon balls fly through the air, making little noise, until they disappear into the water with a small splash.

Before the next maneuver, another volley of cannon smoke can be seen before the sound of the explosions could be heard.

The maneuver begins, and the cannon balls hit the water closer this time, but still away from the current path of the ship.

Oliver watches the Captain, waiting for a signal.

Captain Levi waits, waits, then nods to Oliver.

"New maneuver! Hard to port ten seconds!" Oliver yells to the whole crew.

The cannons fire again; the sound travels faster now that the ship has closed some distance.

The cannon balls land in the water where the previous maneuver would have left the ship had they turned when they had practiced.

"You knew," you say to Captain Levi.

He acknowledges your statement with a small nod, never taking his eyes off the port or the cannon locations.

The plan went out the window with the last maneuver, and the whole crew needs to prepare again for another, but not knowing when it will come is nerve racking. The land wall approaches too, getting closer and closer, which means they would have to halt the ship at some point. You hope it won't be in the sightline of a cannon.

Another volley of cannon fire and another maneuver is called. This time the cannon balls land close to the ship, close enough to cause some crew members to step back from their posts on the side of the ship.

"Almost there! Deploy the drogues!" Oliver yells.

Two crew members at the back of the ship throw the large canvas drogues over the edge into the water on long lines, letting the water open them and begin to slow the ship.

"Heave to!" Oliver yells.

The shore is getting dangerously close, but the cannons have silenced for now. The whole crew is focused on the task at hand, turning the sails into the wind, filling them and slowing the ship.

"It's still too fast," Captain Levi says as he contemplates the last measure.

"Drop the anchor!" he yells as the shore approaches.

Tom stands by the capstan, ready to drop the anchor but freezes.

"Drop it now!" Captain Levi yells.

This time, Tom releases the capstan, dropping the anchor fast. The capstan spins and everyone stays clear as to not be smacked by it.

The anchor hits bottom and pulls a little more line. The ship jerks closer to a halt, but the bottom scrapes can be heard till the ship comes to a full stop, half due to the anchor and the other half hitting hard on the bottom.

"Prepare the ship to move!" Captain Levi calls out. In case a cannon fires, it won't be able to take the hits.

But nothing sounds. It is quiet, quieter than anyone would be comfortable with, but the crew moves, preparing the ship.

The port has been walled in, and the ship had come to rest near the far-left side of where the entrance would be.

Captain Levi maintains a wary eye toward the top of the wall, waiting for someone or something to peek over.

Some time passes before the top of a ladder peaks over the wall.

A face appears over the wall. It's surveying the ship.

"What do you want?" the man yells.

"It's Levi. I'm here to speak to the Harbormaster and Philip," Captain Levi hollers back at the man.

"Levi!" the man yells back. "I thought you were done with this place!"

"Many things were said, but if I could have a few moments with Philip and the Harbormaster, we'll be back on our way," Captain Levi responds, maintaining his composure.

At this, the face disappears behind the wall.

After some time, another face appears.

"Levi! What do you want?" This voice is less harsh, but still short and to the point.

"Philip! It is good to hear your voice! Like I told the individual before, I'd like to speak to you and the Harbormaster if it isn't too much trouble," Captain Levi responds.

"Well, I'm right here. Speak," Philip responds.

"*And* the Harbormaster. I promise it won't take long, and we'll be gone as quickly as we came."

Philip looks down at the ship and thinks for a long moment. He yells down at those below him, calling for something.

After a short time, he throws a large rope over the wall.

"Come on then," Philip yells, disappearing behind the wall.

Captain Levi breathes a sigh of relief.

"And that was the easy part," he jests, cracking a small smile.

Tom pops up from below deck.

"We're taking on water!" he says before disappearing again.

"Oliver, evaluate that and get started fixing what you can. We'll be back as quickly as possible," Captain Levi says, looking to you to follow.

You follow the captain to the ship's boat, to row over to the wall.

As they are lowering the two of you into the water, you have to ask, "Why am I coming with you?"

Captain Levi readies one oar, while you get the other, thinking on the response.

"You need to see what I believe we are going to find," the captain says.

"What's that?" you ask.

"A hostage," he replies.

The small boat hits the water, and you row to the wall where the rope is dangling down.

The climb up is easy enough. Time on ships these last few years has made you strong, and something like this, while unimaginable before, comes much easier to you.

At the top of the wall, you survey the harbor or lack of harbor. There is no water; it has all been drained out. The remnants of coral and seabed can be seen across where the small bay should be. In its place grass has grown down into the lowest parts. Kids can be seen playing, rolling down the hill to the bottom by the wall and then hiking back up again to do it all over.

Captain Levi shakes his head at the sight and moves to take the ladder down the other side of the wall. You follow close behind him.

At the bottom, you are met by Philip, Captain Levi sticks out his hand to shake, and Philip pauses, looking at the hand, almost as if he has forgotten the ritual. He puts his hand forward to shake.

"Thank you for letting us visit," Captain Levi says, ignoring the welcome cannons that tried to sink us on our way in.

"Of course. We were quite surprised to see who it was, not expecting you to ever show up here again," Philip says.

"Me too, Philip. Me too, but the Harbormaster asked me to visit, and so here I am," Captain Levi responds as he surveys the surrounding area and the town.

"You have made some significant changes since I was here last. I'm a little confused in walling in the harbor. Doesn't that defeat the purpose of being a harbor?"

Philip takes a moment to respond to the question.

"It wasn't in use, and after the attack and the outside threats continuing to grow, the decision was made to wall it off."

"We would have liked to use it," Captain Levi says, taking in a breath and exhaling the additional thoughts he wanted to verbalize. "We should be getting to the Harbormaster. I don't want to take any more of your time."

"Of course. I'm sure you know the way, but I'll walk you," Philip says starting off toward the town's center.

The people in the Golden Harbor look like those in other harbors, but something about their attitude and demeanor was different, more standoffish. In other harbors, people seemed to have a natural curiosity about visitors, wanting to hear their stories and find out all about them. Sometimes in other harbors the curiosity was seen as a little too much, but here in the Golden Harbor, it seemed more like an extreme disinterest, almost a disdain that they would be bothered with these two new individuals.

Not everyone though. There were those that smiled at the sight of new people; they still maintained that desire to welcome anyone to the harbor.

"There was a time when everyone was welcoming in this place," Captain Levi whispers to you as you both follow Philip. "Outward facing, looking toward the sea. Then it grew, and they kept building. First it was things that served the mission, things that would help put others to sea. Eventually, the things being built were said to help the mission, but it was for the harbor. That is when I left. I spoke up, and it wasn't appreciated."

"You wanted us to tear it all down." Philip says. Having heard Captain Levi's words, he moves back to walk with us the rest of the way to the Harbormaster's building.

"I'm sure now that I was wrong in my delivery Philip, but I won't apologize for what I was trying to warn you against. What I said was going to happen, did happen here," Captain Levi says with conviction.

Philip thinks on it for a moment.

"This is where I know we will never agree. We have a strong population here, a productive population. How many times did others come attacking us for that strength? How many times did they come expecting us to solve their problems?" Philip's rebuttal is sound.

He continues, "You come now to tell us we are doing it all wrong, like the others before you. Why should we listen to you?"

Captain Levi walks for a moment, thinking.

"The strength of the population is great. You are productive, but for what? When was the last time you added one to your numbers outside of childbirth? Brought one out of the sea into this life?"

The conversation has reached a stalemate as you approach the Harbormaster's office. Philip pulls out a key and unlocks a padlock holding chains on the door.

"You're kidding, right?" Captain Levi says. "What do you think you are doing locking Him up, tell me how that is productive?"

Captain Levi pushes past Philip as he opens the door. You follow him, and Philip follows behind.

For being locked away, the foyer is clean and well kept. Captain Levi walks past the main stairs and to the library where he remembers the Harbormaster works from in this harbor.

The first thing you notice is the sound of birds, a few cooing doves are heard, but upon entering and disturbing the peace of the room, several begin to hop around their cages.

The Harbormaster is at the far end of the room at His desk affixing a small piece of paper to a dove's leg. As He finishes, He looks up to see you.

"Ah good, you're here!" the Harbormaster says while releasing the dove into the air.

The bird takes flight, circling the room a few times before flying out of an open skylight in the ceiling.

"Philip, it has been a moment. Will you be joining us? You are more than welcome to stay. In fact, I would like that very much," the Harbormaster requests.

"Much to do, sir. Much to do," Philip says as he turns to leave.

"Of course. I'm always here when you have more time," the Harbormaster says as Philip closes the door.

The Harbormaster's head falls, sad from the encounter, but always hopeful. He looks up at you both.

"I'm so glad to see you two." The Harbormaster smiles, getting up, as He comes in for a big hug.

The next hour or so is one you'll never forget. The conversation, the encouragement, some questions answered, never all. At a point during a lull in the conversation, Captain Levi asks about the chains on the door.

"Why don't you leave? If they keep you locked up, letting you out when it pleases them, why stay?" Levi asks.

The Harbormaster smiles at the question.

"Because there are those that need and want me here and come seek me out. I still send my commissions, albeit in a less conventional manner," He says, getting up to walk to the cages and feed some of the birds.

"They can lock the doors all they want, but I'm never as stuck as they think. They can present me how they wish, but it doesn't change Me, or who I Am.

That is something many have failed at over the years and will continue to fail, because I Am who I Am. And any who seek Me out will find that about Me."

The Harbormaster retrieves another dove out of the cage and carries it back to His desk.

"Doesn't it bother you?" you ask. "When they present You in a way that is counter to who You are."

"If you are asking if I get angry, the answer is yes. If you are asking if it makes Me sad, the answer is yes. I don't know if I would say one happens more than the other. All I've ever wanted was to have a friendship with each and every one of them. So, if I get that opportunity, I am happy, but to experience one, you have to understand the other. There are those who will reject me or forget me."

The Harbormaster writes on a piece of paper as the dove waits at His desk.

"Philip knows what he must do. We have discussed in length, but there are those in the harbor that reject that plan and won't allow him to do what must be done," the Harbormaster says, reading over what He has written then rolling it up and affixing it to the dove before letting it go, flying up and away through the same skylight as before.

"And what is that?" Captain Levi asks.

"Turn those blasted cannons on that wall and destroy it, stack gunpowder in the wall and blow it up. Lasso a whale and ram the wall down." The Harbormaster roars with laughter before calming and getting to the point. "Remove the wall, and use the harbor for what it was intended."

Captain Levi begins to speak but is cut off.

"I know what you are going to offer, and it can't come from you. If you attack that wall, they will rebuild it, and it will reinforce their reasoning for having it in the first place," the Harbormaster says, sitting back in His large chair.

"They were attacked you know, because of me... because of the work We do..." The Harbormaster looks off remembering the day. "It was tragic but presented an amazing opportunity to reach out to those who attacked and try and bridge the gap that existed, but some of those in the harbor wouldn't have it and decided to build the wall. They convinced others in the harbor to support it. And here We are."

The three of you sit for a moment, taking it in.

"So Philip doesn't want the wall?" Captain Levi asks.

"No more than you or I, but he has to pick his battles, and while he does that, the wall continues to grow." The Harbormaster sighs and smiles a small somber smile. "Be gentle with Philip. He is trying more than you know."

The time has come for you both to leave, and after several hugs and encouraging words, the Harbormaster ushers the two of you to the door.

"Don't be strangers. Ask Philip for a flag to fly on your way in so they don't try and sink you again. I'm so glad they missed." The Harbormaster laughs.

"Us too," Captain Levi says shaking the Harbormaster's hand.

You do the same, and the Harbormaster pulls you in for one last hug, whispering in your ear as He gets close.

"Don't worry about Charlie. He will be okay." He pulls away from the hug, smiling at the confusion on your face. "All this way to visit us, and the most important mission is playing out on your ship as we speak. Such a good day!"

Even in your confusion, you can't help but smile back at the Harbormaster, thinking maybe being locked up has made Him senile.

"Goodbye, sir," you say as you walk out the door, closing it behind you.

Philip is waiting for the two of you as you exit.

"Did you get everything you needed?" he asks.

Captain Levi smiles at the question.

"Yeah, Philip we did. I want to apologize for leaving the way I did back then. That can't have been easy to carry that load by yourself, and I'm sorry."

Philip's face shows intrigue and surprise, but he fights it off with a mild grimace.

"It wasn't, isn't, but I appreciate the apology. Apology accepted."

Silence holds the air creating an awkward moment.

Philip breaks it by holding out a small package to Captain Levi, wrapped in paper.

"What's this?" Captain Levi asks as he grabs it, but Philip doesn't let go yet.

"A flag. You can fly it if you'd like to return, so long as you promise not to attack the harbor." Philip holds on to the package waiting for the words.

"I promise, Philip. Just visits, no attacks."

Philip releases the package to Captain Levi who holds onto it.

"Thank you. It does mean a lot to me," Captain Levi says.

The walk back down to the boat is quiet, but the tension from the walk up is gone, and there is an understanding now. The two old friends shake hands and part ways on a much better foundation.

Captain Levi ascends the ladder on the way out and back down the rope on the other side without saying much.

Back on the small ship boat, as you begin to row, he pipes up.

"Even after all this time, I still need reminding that these missions can last a lifetime before you see the progress you want. I have a feeling that this is going to be one of those," Captain Levi says as he watches the wall move away.

"Sometimes, I think those are the best ones." You finish rowing to the ship and help attach the ropes so it can be hauled back aboard.

Once back on ship, you see Tom staring at you wide-eyed with a big smile on his face.

"Look who helped us patch the ship!" Tom says, while pointing over to someone sitting on the deck, still a little wet from being in the water.

"Charlie!" you say, stealing Tom's thunder as he was about to say who it was too.

You run over, hugging Charlie as he stands, almost knocking him over.

"It is so good to see you! What happened? How'd you find us?" You unleash several questions before Tom reels you back in.

"He was in the neighborhood and saw we needed help patching the outside, so he offered. I invited him aboard to wait for you, because I said you wouldn't forgive me if I didn't make him wait to see you," Tom fills you in.

"I wouldn't have. It is so good to see you. Will you sail with us for a bit? You don't have to stay, but I'd like it if you sailed with us for a bit?" you ask.

"Sure, I think I can do that," Charlie says, without the reluctance that has followed him before.

The crew sets about their jobs and hurries around the ship. Tom darts off to see to his duties, and you walk with Charlie around the ship.

"You know the Harbormaster said I'd find you down here. I thought he may have been crazy, but here you are. I want you to know that you can stay as long as you'd like. You can come back to the harbor with us, no strings, a step toward something new."

"I've seen the harbors, been in them. Nothing special, you know," Charlie says.

"Oh, you're right about that, the buildings, the materials, wood, clay, metal, gold; nothing special about that at all. The people are what make it special. The people are what make it a harbor, everyone coming together with the Harbormaster on a common mission to send out these ships, going where the people are, going to find them."

Charlie listens to you speak.

"Which is funny, because you have found me more than I've found you, but I believe that is for a reason. You told me before that you were looking for something. I think you found it, but no matter how many times you find the same thing, you run away again and again. And I don't know why that is, but it keeps leading you back to the same place."

Charlie remains silent.

"What I'm saying is maybe you try staying this time. See what happens. Not because I'm asking you to, but because you want to." You make your case.

Charlie thinks about it for a moment and nods his head in affirmation.

"Good. Let's get you something to eat," you say as the ship's sails unfurl and the long trek home begins.

The size of the harbor isn't the issue; neither is the wealth of the harbor. They dealt with some severe events and that led them down a new path. One where they decided to close themselves off to the rest of the world. Their main purpose was neglected, impossible to carry out at this point. For churches and organizations, what does this look like?

Many organizations understand the need for inward-facing activities as well as outward-facing activities to ensure the customers are being served. This is where churches differ because the funds that fuel the mission of the church are coming from those who attend the church. From the inside, they fund the mission of the church that reaches to those outside of the church.

The issue we see in the Golden Harbor is one where the organization decides to shift from an outward focus to an inward focus in how they care for and spend the wealth they've been given. Instead of seeking out the lost and funding the missions of those in the harbor as they are called by the Harbormaster, they spend their funds on other things, self-serving things.

The last thing I want is to load up a cannon myself and take shots at churches and organizations that this may apply to. But it is critical to evaluate not only yourself, but the organization you are a part of. An inward-facing marriage, inward-facing job, or inward-facing existence is going to be lonely. You may get everything *you* want, but at some point, you will look outward, and when you do, you may find there is no one there with you. They will have all left because you were too consumed with yourself and your own desires.

As you evaluate, you first need to ensure you have some baseline data in place. We've discussed this at length earlier, but know your mission. This is critical to even began evaluating any other aspect. Once you're sure about the mission, figure out what it means to be "winning" at the mission. How do you keep score? How can you measure success?

Some people get all bent out of shape when you mention metrics and numbers, especially when it comes to their church, but as Christians we were given pretty clear instructions as to what we're supposed to be doing. Matthew 28:19-20 says, "Therefore go and make disciples of all nations, baptizing them in the name of the Father and of the Son and of the Holy Spirit, and teaching them to obey everything I have commanded you..." If we haven't done that at all, of course, we resist measurement—it reminds us of how far we've drifted from the Great Commission. It makes me feel terrible when I evaluate myself and my lack of effort over the years to be intentional with my mission, whether it is my writing or my discipleship of young men or spending quality time with my daughters, raising them to be godly young women. I'm right there with you. It is never too late to start figuring out what winning at your mission looks like and start keeping score.

There's another truth this chapter reveals: the omnipresence of God. Up to this point, we'd hinted at other Harbormasters but had only seen the Harbormaster in our home harbor. Here He appears again—locked behind walls, yet still sending doves and commissioning sailors. His nature never changes. His will never changes. His love for us never changes. When we encounter "different" Harbormasters from harbor to harbor, we're not meeting a different God; we're seeing another facet of the same flawless diamond. In this world we can feel like we are meeting a new person, but He remains the same.

The Golden Harbor tried to lock Him away in order to portray Him when and how they desired to fit their narrative. But He cannot be contained, and His work continued despite their attempted jailing. They became so consumed with their own status and presence that they forgot who He is. May we never grow so inward that we believe our limited view can fully encompass His limitless presence.

Where can I go from your Spirit? Where can I flee from your presence? If I go up to the heavens, you are there; if I make my bed in the depths, you are there. If I rise on the wings of the dawn, if I settle on the far side of the sea, even there your hand will guide me, your right hand will hold me fast.

Psalm 139:7-10

REUNITED

The ship, steady and sure, cuts through the waters that once threatened to drown you on your way back to home harbor. Tom nudges you, pointing over to Charlie sitting near the railing watching the water as it streams by. You make your way to him and sit down beside.

"We can make twelve knots with the right wind," you say watching the water with him.

"Fast," Charlie says, watching the water as if he can see right through it down into the depths and everything he is giving up. The entire weight of a life lived under the waves silently crushing him.

"What is it?" you ask.

"I can't do this." Charlie looks to you.

"You are doing it, right here as we sit. I'm watching you do it."

Charlie looks back to the water.

You let the silence hang and chime back in. "The pressure of that life, the pains from it, the joys, the friends, the family. It's part of who we are, and I know it feels like by saying no to it, you are saying no to all the good things from it. But what you can offer to them is so much greater now: the warmth, the love, the air. All the things that they need more, and you can help them find it. He is always looking for them, right there waiting for them to come. You can be a part of that."

It sits with Charlie for a moment.

"Or you can jump back in. It's always our choice, but I hope and pray you stay on the boat with us. I have so many people I want you to meet."

You squeeze his shoulder as you stand up. "You know how many people Tom and I tell about you? They think we're making it up like we were dehydrated or something, imagining you. This crazy guy jumping into our boat in the middle of the ocean. You gotta stay long enough to prove that for us... It's the least you could do."

Charlie chuckles at the joke and looks back toward the water.

You leave him to his thoughts as you wander back to Tom.

"He going to be okay?" Tom asks still concerned about the whole situation.

"He's in it right now, just needs to decide. Pray for him, Tom. Just pray."

Tom pats you on the back and heads to the crow's nest on the main mast. His favorite place to be alone for such a task.

You watch Charlie as he watches the water, like by some other power you can see the storm raging inside of him.

In your vision, Charlie stands on a small ships deck being pummeled by a storm, the waves taking the shape of several different faces and scenes from his past, never long enough to make them out, but Charlie knows each one before it appears and lashes at the ship breaking pieces of the boat one by one. Charlie tries to fix them as they break, running about the deck fighting with every ounce of his being to make it work, but by the time one thing is fixed, five more have broken. He wants to give up so badly; he wants to give in. It is so hard for him. Every time you think he is finished, he pulls himself up and goes again and again and again. He rages back at the storm, screaming obscenities into darkness and crying out for it to stop. But nothing is working, nothing at all.

Finally, amid all the rage and misery, anger and hate and bitterness, you hear but a whisper.

"Lord, please!"

The storm continues to rage, and the waves rock the boat. Then—silence. All sound falls away and the whisper continues.

"Lord, please!"

Everything is chaos, the sea around the boat, the wind ripping across the water, but still no sound.

"Lord..."

Tears fall harder than any bit of rain from the storm. It's all background to the immensity of the transformation happening before you.

Charlie falls to his knees sobbing, a broken man able to face the truth of it all.

As you watch in silent reverence, you see a figure appear in the boat, walking over to Charlie and picking him up. He hugs Charlie and whispers several things to him. The storm subsides a little, but not fully. Those faces and past life experiences in the waves are even less recognizable, but still there.

As if time flows forward, you watch as the figure and Charlie begin to work on the boat together even amid the storm. They fix different parts of the boat; the mast, wheel, and then Charlie stumbles breaking things they just fixed. Without judgement He hugs Charlie, and they set about fixing them again. The storm subsides as Charlie seems to grow older. The two of them sail together. In a matter of minutes, you've viewed a lifetime on this ship of Charlie's. Good times and bad, storms and sunny skies. All of it with this new Shipmate.

You find yourself back by the helm watching Charlie. The worry plastered across his face is gone, and he seems to have a peace about him. Even a smile creeps across his lips as he discreetly wipes tears from eyes.

"Land ho!" Tom yells down from the crow's nest.

The rest of the crew cheers at the news. Home for some, rest for others, but sanctuary for all.

Everyone knows their part to play as they bring the ship in, but Captain Levi calls out orders to make sure nothing is forgotten.

A larger boat is in the harbor, and you recognize it. The *Koinónia* sits moored at the docks, a few laborers milling about it fixing pieces of a sail and loading various supplies. You haven't seen the ship since that day it pulled you from the deep.

Charlie sees the boat and begins scanning the docks as if looking for something.

"That's the boat that pulled me out," you say as Charlie stares hard at everyone around the boat. "I haven't seen it since it brought me to this harbor. I'll have to introduce you to Carson. He is a riot."

"It has been so long, but it hasn't changed at all," Charlie says looking at the ship sitting there.

"What do you mean?" you ask.

Charlie is about to respond, but he has found the thing he was looking for. Or the person.

Standing on the shore, overseeing the loading of supplies is the captain, Charlie's father.

Charlie jumps to the dock, moving toward the man he hasn't seen in years. Halfway there, he pauses, flooded with the thoughts of a possible rejection or hate that could come.

By this time, you've caught up and are moving behind Charlie, watching him watch his father.

The captain turns, looking over at your ship and then to you. A big smile crosses his face as he recognizes you, but then he looks to Charlie, a tinge of recognition gives birth to a totality of emotions. He drops the papers in his hand and begins walking toward Charlie, his speed increases until he is running.

He reaches Charlie and with not even a hint of anger, he wraps his big arms around him and holds him.

"My son!" the captain beams.

Charlie is crying now and the captain too. You may or may not shed a few tears in the moment. When Tom recalls the story, he found you blubbering like a baby watching the embrace.

The captain and Charlie share several hushed exchanges, and at the end of it, the captain looks over to you, pointing at you and breaking into even more tears. He moves to you, grabs you for a huge hug as well.

"Thank you for bringing my boy back to me."

You don't know what to say. Any words that begin to take shape are swallowed with the lump in your throat. You nod in acknowledgement and hug the captain back. He pulls his son into the embrace, and you find you're all hugging now.

"Ahem..." Tom coughs, interrupting the embrace after what seems like too long to him. "I helped..."

The levity breaks up the embrace, and everyone laughs.

"Where is Carson? I want him to meet Tom," you ask, scanning the *Koinónia's* crew.

"You mean Captain Carson of the *Toioutos*," the captain says with a big smile.

"Captain? Of his own ship?" you ask.

"That is a story that may take some time." The captain says.

"We have a few things to finish up, but I want to hear it, yeah?" you say, looking back to the crew doing all the work getting the ship settled in port. But none looking upset about your reunion. Captain Levi smiles at the exchange, knowing this is what it is all about.

"Of course," the captain says, and he pulls his son in close again. They walk back to where his first mate has gathered up the manifest paperwork and is trying to sort it all out.

You turn with Tom and walk back to the ship.

"What's happier than happy?" Tom asks as you walk.

"I don't know, joyful maybe, gleeful... ecstatic?" you opine.

"Oh, good word, EC-STAT-IC." Tom looks back at the captain before continuing. "Such a good day."

"The best," you agree.

"I love my life." Tom climbs aboard, jogging over to help with some tangled ropes.

You look back at the captain and then to the ship, Tom and the crew. "Me too," you almost whisper. "Me too."

Every now and again we all need moments when we stop long enough to look back—and realize we're living in the miracle of God's design. Seeing the way everything moved and orchestrated to bring us to where we are today, we have a moment of extreme clarity. A moment of EC-STAT-IC joy! When is the last time you stopped to do that?

If you haven't in a while, look back on those pillars in your life that were pivotal in bringing you to where you are today. Those things that you can now recognize as a defining moment or choice that was made that brought you here.

Not all of them are happy moments, and if we are honest with ourselves, some of them were very painful or took place due to poor decisions on our part.

Watching Charlie sit there, struggling through the past demons haunting him and ripping at any progress he made in his life is tough. Anyone with someone in their life who has dealt or is still dealing with the pain of a past knows how hard it is to watch them go through that. We all have the capacity to do that in our own lives. Holding onto the things that we regret or the decisions we made. Even living in the past because we long for "the good ole days" instead of what we may have to face now in this moment.

If you've read this far, then you may remember the conversation the captain had with you early in the book. The captain wasn't chasing his son—he was obeying his call. And in doing so, he found everything he thought he'd lost. It is difficult in the moment to have clarity on this point. It isn't until we look back over the course of a year, five, ten years even, before you can see the movements that took place to bring you to where you are today. Even when setting a well-planned course for our lives, rarely does it go as we planned. The captain had no idea that placing himself where he was supposed to be brought him to you, which brought you to his son, which brought his son back to him.

God does have perfect plans for all of us. Notice I didn't say joyful or painless, but perfect. Looking over the course of time and space, even to the astronomical odds that lead to me typing on this keyboard today, blows me away. I urge you to take some time and think back on how you got to where you are right now. Life moves so fast that if we don't take those moments to recognize God's hand in our lives, we may keep missing it all—and how sad would that be? Take time today to look back. You may just find that the God who brought you this far is still writing something beautiful with your life.

"[B]eing confident of this, that he who began a good work in you will carry it on to completion until the day of Christ Jesus."
Philippians 1:6

The End... is Just the Beginning

You're having a heck of a time refinishing the deck of this old ship. A few days after returning to port, you received another commission. This old schooner has been sitting in the harbor for years, and now it is your job to see it returned to its former glory.

Sanding the deck, grinding the boards down, peeling away years of salt, sun, and neglect, until you find the shape they were meant to hold was a slow process. The main deck area went easier and faster overall, but several places along the way have slowed progress where you have to stop and rethink how you'll sand edging or replace a broken piece where needed.

The process is time-consuming and hard to see an end to the work. As thoughts creep in about your task at hand, you remember the road you've been on. Even with the sweat and blood and hard work from refinishing a deck, you know and believe so much more will come of it, especially thinking back on helping Charlie and Tom find their way to where the Harbormaster wanted them to be.

If you accomplished nothing else during your time, you would be happy with that. That you got to play a part in a small way with eternal outcomes, that process, that opportunity far surpasses any dreams you may have or possible ideas bouncing around in your head.

We think at times that the most important jobs are that of the captain of the *Life Bringer*, or the one who leads the harbor in the construction of hundreds of ships, but to stand back and watch the workings of the entire system, you see how each and every small role enables the whole community to work. The owner of a bar, the mail man, various shipmates and countless others. These people had a profound effect on all of us and our journeys. We are all different because of it, all the better and more different. They all helped you work on the rough edges, the broken pieces lifted out and replaced. But still we look to these large figures, expecting everything amazing to flow from them, when in fact it is the small everyday tasks of common people that shaped the world you've enjoyed. The way they approached their tasks with a joy and peace you didn't expect to find in the ordinary. But it was there, quietly changing you. Showing you what living looks like and you're happier because of it.

Over the side of the boat, you hear someone climbing up the drydock ladder. Tom peeks over.

"Permission to come aboard captain?" he jokes.

"Granted," you reply, standing up and stretching out your back.

"She is going to be a beauty," Tom says, looking the boat over.

"Yeah, I think she has some years left in her," you say while giving the main mast a rap with your fist.

"The ship is leaving soon, and I wanted to..." Tom pauses, emotion flooding in.

You put up a hand letting him know it is fine.

"I know, Tom," you say.

He hands you a piece of paper, a small commission.

"I didn't tell you about it. I should have told you sooner. But I didn't want to burden you while you were carrying so much already."

You open it up and read it, tears welling up in your eyes.

My dearest Tom,

As you set sail for the Golden Harbor with Captain Levi, I need you to carry out another mission for me. A very important mission. Charlie is in that area and needs our help. If possible, can you see to it that the ship is damaged a bit? I know this is a lot to ask, but Charlie has always had a helping heart, and if the ship is damaged, he'll come to your aid. This opportunity is critical for him. I know you'll do your best.

The Harbormaster

You lower the paper, and for a moment, everything around you disappears. The sound of gulls, the creak of timber, even Tom's breathing—all of it fades. You close your eyes and think, *He knew. All Along.* You open your eyes and smile.

"Wait, so you wrecked the ship on purpose?" You laugh, handing the commission back to Tom.

"He told me to!" He chuckles, defending himself.

You pull Tom in for hug.

"Be good brother. Go find that girl," you say releasing him.

"I'll be seeing you," Tom says as he climbs back over the side and down the ladder.

You watch as he walks toward the docks to board his ship. Waving one last time, he looks back.

With a big smile on your face, you get back down on all fours and start sanding the deck again, knowing this is where you're supposed to be.

You'll be waiting and watching for the next great adventure that you're blessed to be a part of, but for now, this deck is it.

Until We Sail Again

Thank you for joining me on this voyage. As I said at the very beginning, there were seasons in my walk with God when I wrestled deeply with questions of grace and calling. Through these stories—anchored in His Word—I found answers.

Some of you have just broken the surface, drawing in the first full breath of fresh air in a long time. Others are wary of harbor life, still mending from the hurt of a past port. Some have been sailing for years yet can't remember the last soul you helped pull from the water. And yet, here you are—alive, called, and needed.

You may feel unworthy. You may believe your course has drifted too far, or that your past has closed every harbor to you. But grace has already found you. The Harbormaster Himself has called you aboard—not because of what you have done, but because of who He is. Once rescued, you are called to become a rescuer.

If you're unsure whether you've even left the depths, let me be as clear as the open horizon: the Man who pulls people from the water—Jesus—died on the cross for the sins of the world: yours, mine, everyone's. No good work can lift you from the waters. Only this—accept the gift of His sacrifice. Romans 10:9 says, "If you declare with your mouth, 'Jesus is Lord,' and believe in your heart that God raised him from the dead, you will be saved."

From there, your next steps are simple: open His Word—the Bible. Spend time with the Harbormaster—God—in prayer. Learn His charts. Follow His compass. Let His truth fill your sails and set your course toward those still adrift.

You do not sail alone. As you close these pages, I pray you find a harbor—church—you can call home. And from there, launch your ship—ministry—with purpose into the waters ahead, eyes fixed on the horizon, and a heart ready to answer when He asks, *"Will you go?"*

Before You Disembark...

Your voyage with *Parables of the Sea* means the world to me.
If this story stirred your heart, would you help other readers set sail by leaving a short review wherever you found the book—Barnes & Noble, Lifeway, Amazon, or your favorite bookstore? Your words—even just a sentence or two—carry this message farther than you can imagine.

   And if the journey moved you, share your favorite moment on social media and tag **@SeaAndSoulPress** so we can sail together and spread the word.

About the Author

Justin J Major is a Christian husband, father of two, war veteran, mentor, and church elder. He has served the country since the age of eighteen—first in the U.S. Army, and now as an intelligence analyst for the federal government. Justin lives in Texas with his wife and youngest daughter, where he serves as an elder at Lifepoint Fellowship Church in Tyler.

A lifelong storyteller, Justin writes to share narratives of grace that inspire spiritual growth and transformation. His debut novel, *Parables of the Sea*, blends allegory and devotion, inviting readers to navigate life's storms with faith and purpose. Through the ministry of Sea & Soul Press, he continues to craft works that call believers to live out the Great Commission with courage and hope.

Connect with Justin at **seaandsoulpress.com**. Sign up for the newsletter ("Crew Updates") and receive a full, never-before-seen story from the world of *Parables of the Sea as well as* devotionals, new releases, and behind-the-scenes looks at what is next.

ON THE HORIZON

Beyond familiar shores lies a new voyage—one entrusted not to the seasoned, but to the young. In *The Young Captain's Commission*, a surprising call from the Harbormaster sends Carson and a handful of unlikely leaders into waters others believe they are too inexperienced to navigate. With courage tested and friendships forged, their mission will challenge what they—and the world around them—believe about calling, faith, and the measure of a true captain.